THE COST OF A
SPARROW

ERIC WATSON

Scripture quotations marked KJV are from the Holy Bible, King James Version (Authorized Version). First published in 1611. Quoted from the KJV Classic Reference Bible, Copyright © 1983 by The Zondervan Corporation.

Printed in the United States of America.

Library of Congress Control Number: 2020914091

ISBN   Paperback   978-1-64803-301-8
              Hardback   978-1-64803-302-5
              eBook   978-1-64803-308-7

Westwood Books Publishing LLC
11416 SW Aventino Drive
Port Saint Lucie, FL 34987

www.westwoodbookspublishing.com

Are not two sparrows sold for a farthing?
And one of these shall not fall to the ground
without your Father. Matt. 10:29. KJV.

Illustrations by Jill Watson.

Chapter 1

Because of Boots

I can hardly believe that it was only last Sunday that all this began; it seems ages and yet it really was only five days ago. When we got back from church at one o'clock, there was no sign of Boots. We called to him and when he didn't come we rattled a spoon on his enamel dinner plate, but even this had no effect. He usually meets us in the drive when he hears the car drive up and if he doesn't, then the spoon on the plate trick flushes him out from wherever he is and from whatever he has been doing. He would never miss the opportunity of a meal.

Boots is mostly Australian terrier and he gets his name from two perfectly marked front feet, which are snowy white, instead of his basic black and brown. He's the most adorable, but mischievous dog that ever there was. He's not a puppy and I don't think he ever was. Dad says he's about two years old, but we can't be certain because he came from the R.S.P.C.A pound at Ballarat. Mum thinks his original owners dumped him because he was smarter than they were and I can believe that; he really is very bright. Shirley thinks that like the Gaddarene swine in the Bible, he's possessed by a destructive spirit and if you could have seen what he did to the slippers given to Dad on his birthday, you might believe it too.

My name is Elaine and I'm just eleven years old. In fact, that's how our story began; with my eleventh birthday and the gift that Dad and Mum gave me, which was Boots. I'm certain that if it hadn't

1

been for him, then none of this would have happened. Well, to be honest, it would have happened all right, but to somebody else, not us. I keep trying to convince Dad that if it hadn't been for Boots, the whole course of history could have been changed. He laughs and says that we exaggerate our adventures and that they grow in the telling like fishermen's tales of the fish they catch. Dad only comes in to the adventures at the very end, when things have to be cleared up, so he doesn't know how we suffer while it's taking place. Not that we really suffer, it's very exciting at the time. Geraldine says it's all 'kids stuff', when she's trying to act grown-up, but she gets just as excited as the rest of us when we're in the thick of it.

It might help you to understand how we see things, if first, I tell you something about ourselves, before I tell you what took place. It really makes a lot of difference. To start with, we're P.K's, that's preacher's kids. Dad is Pastor of the church at Olney, in the central highlands of Victoria, near Ballarat and 'we', are his family. I often wonder how the five children of one male and one female can be so different; but we are and I also think at times, that I am the only completely sane member of the family, especially when we are involved in an adventure like this was.

We are all 'born-again' Christians and we know that everything that happens to us is part of God's plan and purpose for our lives, but we also know that He has given us wisdom, commonsense and free will to act for ourselves. This is where our troubles often begin.

I love my sister Geraldine very much, but sometimes she can be a big pain in the neck. She's two years older than I am and has all the advantages of a year at High School and she sure likes to give us all the benefit of her great experience. You'll see what I mean no doubt, as the story unfolds. Shirley, on the other hand, is two years younger than I am and just at that difficult age where she thinks she knows everything. To make matters worse, she thinks that the things she knows nothing about just don't exist, which makes for frustration quite often, believe me! My youngest sister, Rachel, is a sweetie, but she's only seven years old. She's so trusting and so optimistic about life and everything in it. I know that I shouldn't have favourites, so I don't, but if I did, my favourite sister would be Rachel. That only leaves Timothy, who's five, but since he's a boy and since he's sick anyway, he hardly comes into the story at all. So, there we all were, wondering what had become of Boots!

"Maybe he's gone back to his former owners," said Dad and I thought I detected a satisfied smirk.

"Oh no," said Mum, "I can't bear to think about it. Life will never be the same again for me." I didn't know that my mother had any affection for Boots at all and I said so.

"There you are, Rose," smiled Dad, "I told you that sarcasm is wasted on children. They naturally believe every word that their parents utter." Mum smiled now.

"Surely, no-one believes that I like that monster. Why, he's chewed up, just about everything I hold dear in the world. Only this morning he 'killed' my oven glove and buried it in the herb garden."

"Not the herb garden," sighed Dad. "I'd just transplanted over fifty young shoots from the propagator."

That's Boots, I thought, how to win friends and influence people. Never the less, I was worried, because this sort of behaviour was so out of character. It's true, I had only had Boots for two weeks, but in those fourteen days, he'd never once missed a meal, nor missed welcoming me home from school or church. He seemed to have a built-in clock that governed his coming and his going. Never the one to hang about the house, his business took him to all the corners of our twenty-acre property, but he was always to be found somewhere in the drive when my homecoming was imminent.

I told Geraldine that I was going to need her help again. I had to find him before lunch, or he would be starving.

"That brute will never starve," laughed Geraldine, "He'd find someone to take pity on him, wherever he was."

We searched the barn first and then the hayshed, favourite places with Boots, because in a dry summer, we sometimes get a rat or two in the sheds and this looked like it was going to be a dry one. Boots is a great ratter. You should have seen how he treated Mum's oven glove before he buried it. However, he wasn't in any of the outbuildings. We went next, to his favourite spot where he spends hours waiting for rabbits. The blackberry bushes and wild roses teem with rabbits, but unlike rats, Boots never catches any. The trouble is, he gets too excited and as soon as he sights one, he begins to yelp as if he has been scalded and no self-respecting rabbit is going to sit around to see what all the fuss is about, especially if he suspects that he might be the cause of the fuss. Down the hole goes the rabbit and Boots digs frantically where the rabbit disappeared. Meanwhile, the rabbit has re-surfaced elsewhere and is sitting thirty metres away, washing his whiskers and watching Boots scrabbling away in the midst of a miniature dust storm, whilst howling like a banshee.

This spot, which we call 'the dell', is right on the edge of our property and is part of some old gold workings, now grown over with furze and blackberries. The whole area around here is riddled with old workings and Mum is always warning us to keep away from them. Most have been filled in, years ago and only a few are dangerous, being four to five metres deep. Beyond our top paddock, is an area of open scrubland, which extends for about half a kilometre, then begins the plantations of the Forestry Commission. They cover hundreds of acres with closely spaced pine trees. It's a bleak, but beautiful spot.

Boots wasn't in the dell and I hadn't expected him to be. Had he been, he would have heard us calling him and would have come at once, but just as we were leaving to move on to the next of Boot's haunts, Shirley arrived, to tell us that lunch was ready and Mum said to get there right away and get washed up As we turned away from the dell and began to walk back alongside our top fence, Geraldine grabbed my arm.

"I've never seen a car there before," she remarked, "How did it get there?"

Against the dark belt of the pine tree trunks could be seen a white car. It was not an abandoned wreck, because even at this distance, we could see the sunlight gleaming on the paintwork and on the chrome trim.

"It's a Ford Falcon," chirped up Shirley, "and there's a dirt track runs along this edge of the plantation to the Commission's nursery."

I wanted to know how she knew about the track and how she knew it was a Ford Falcon car. It really is amazing the things this child picks up. It's little wonder that Mum often says to Dad, 'not in front of the C.H.I.L.D'. Of course, that doesn't fool any of us any more, because the first one to work it out, told all the others. Even Timothy knows and he's only five.

"You'd be surprised at all the things I know," said Shirley, mysteriously.

"We'll all be surprised in a minute," laughed Geraldine, "Dad will be sent to look for us and you know how cross he gets when he has to come looking for us."

We spent a few seconds looking around for the owners of the car, and then went back to the house for lunch. Sunday lunch isn't one of the greatest meals of the week; there's plenty to eat of course, but it's always a scratch meal because no one has time to prepare anything better. In spring and summer, it's always a cold meal and I do so love a hot one. One thing that is always good, though, is the 'family time' we have at every meal. Once Dad has prayed and asked God's blessing on the food He has provided, then we're free to share our thoughts on any subject at all. Nothing is forbidden as long as it's not what Dad calls 'frivolous'. If we need any advice or encouragement, then Dad or Mum will give it. Today, as is often the case on Sundays, we discussed the sermon that Dad had preached at the morning service and Rachel was very confused about Jesus healing 'divers diseases', which she thought was something they got from staying under the water too long. All thoughts of the mysterious car were driven from my mind and it seemed, from the minds of the others too.

After lunch, since Boots still hadn't turned up, we continued our search for him, but suddenly, I thought of the strange appearance of a car, where I had never seen one before. I felt I had to know more about it. I suggested that we go back and see if the car was still there and if anyone had turned up who might own it. Rachel was with us now and she hadn't seen it at all, so she was very keen. The others agreed and we decided to seek cover in the dell, so that we could watch without being seen ourselves.

When we peered through the Hawthorn hedge that marked this part of our boundary, my heart stopped beating within my chest. There was still not a soul in sight. There stood the car, exactly where it had been before, except that the lid of the trunk was now open.

Chapter 2

————⟨∘/∘/∘⟩————

The Stakeout

"Wowsers," yelped Geraldine, "Somebody must be there. That trunk lid wasn't open before. Someone's been back while we were away. I wonder where they are and what they've been doing?"

"Perhaps they're cutting firewood in the plantation," whispered Rachel.

"That's not allowed," said Shirley, "and in any case, we would be able to hear them if they were using a chain saw or a felling axe."

"What," primped Miss Geraldine, "if they are only picking up small pieces for kindling?"

"Then I don't think they would have come so far out into the wild," answered Shirley, "and in the time that we have been watching, surely we would have seen someone coming or going with arms full of kindling."

That exhausted that subject and we settled down behind a low rise to watch for signs of the owner, or owners, of the vehicle. It was one of those lovely days at the beginning of November, when the sun is warm but not hot and a light breeze was blowing towards us from the plantation, carrying with it, the clean fresh smell of pine resin. After a few minutes of watching, during which absolutely nothing happened, we began to talk of other things.

"That smell," sighed Geraldine, "reminds me of Wendell Brown. It's the 'after-shave' that he uses. I think Dorothy Maine buys him a litre of it every Christmas, but it really is nice and seems to suit his personality."

"Dad says we shouldn't call our teachers by their first names," remarked Rachel, "It doesn't show proper respect."

"He's not my teacher," retorted Geraldine, "and neither is Dorothy Maine. If he was, I would do everything I could to thwart the wiley Dorothy in her evil schemes."

"Oh Geraldine," exclaimed Rachel, "I'm sure Miss Maine isn't evil. She only wants to marry him and I know that most of the girls in your High School would like to do that, any way."

"I know she's not evil, infant," laughed Geraldine, "I was only being dramatic."

"He's very handsome, isn't he," smiled Shirley, "have you noticed how his hair curls over his ears when it needs cutting?"

"Janet Draper asked him for a lock of his hair, last week," said Geraldine, "I nearly died of embarrassment, but he just smiled and told her he was having his hair cut on Thursday and that she could go down to the hairdressers and have as much as she wanted. What a squelch. She was really put down."

"I would never pick up anyone's hair in a barber shop," declared Rachel, "and in any case, I think Daddy's hair is much prettier than Mr. Brown's."

I'm afraid that children of that age don't have an atom of romance in their make-up at all. I must admit, I quite like our head teacher, Mr. Brown, but not because of his obvious good looks, but because of his superior intellect. He's by far, the best teacher I have ever had. He talks to me as if I am an equal, unlike many other adults who treat me as if I am of no consequence in their world. Mr. Brown makes me feel as if he really cares about any opinions I may have on any subject we discuss.

Dad says it's a gift with some people, but that many more could work at it if they cared enough about other people to bother. Dad has it too and Mum. They both know how to make children feel that they have a part in the world and that their opinions matter. My parents are great and I love them heaps. Geraldine broke into my reverie.

"Elaine," she said, "would you mind terribly if we never found old Boots again?"

I had to admit that the excitement of the car's appearance, had driven all thoughts of Boots, completely out of my mind. My, what fickle creatures we mortals are. As I replied, I was thinking how Dad had told us that he had committed each one of us into the care of Jesus and I had done the same with Boots.

I was told how it had been when Timothy arrived. He was born with several physical defects, but the chief one was that he had a hole in his heart. The hospital staff where he was born gave up hope and came to tell Mum not to expect him to live through the night. It always makes me weep when I dwell on her reply. She told them that Timothy was given to her, by the God of all creation, that he was given to her for a particular purpose and was a part of God's greater plan for our lives. Then she turned her face to the wall and praised and thanked God for the gift of Timothy and for the trust that He had placed in her in giving to her this child who needed so much love and care. He lived of course and we all love him so much, all of us. We pray for him daily and know that he was not given to us just to be taken away again. God is so good. I just know that if I trust Jesus for everything that I need, He will always be with me and take care of me.

The sun had been warming me and lost in my thoughts, as I had been, I was almost ready to fall asleep, when suddenly; Rachel grabbed my arm so fiercely that it hurt.

"Look," she gasped.

We spun around in the direction she was pointing and before our eyes, seemingly risen from the depths of the earth; three men were walking away from us towards the car. There was nothing special about them to distinguish them from any others who might be seen in this part of the country, except for the manner of their appearing. One minute the scrub was bare of all life, the next, it was dominated by the three denim-clad figures, slightly to our right and about two thirds of the way across the scrub towards the car. At this distance, the only means of recognition was that one of them was slightly taller than the other two and one of those was slightly fatter than his companion. They appeared to be about Mr. Brown's age, that is, mid to late thirties, but it was difficult to tell from the back. They weren't older though, because their walk was vigorous, like a young man who knows where he is going.

We were spellbound, hardly daring to breathe, though it was nonsense of course, to imagine that we could be heard at that distance. I was glad, suddenly, that Boots wasn't with us, because he would have been off, over the scrub, to harass them all the way to their car. Boots hates strangers.

When they arrived at the car, they stopped and looked all around the area; especially it seemed to me, in our direction. We froze and did our level best to look like trees. I was glad that none of us was dressed in bright clothes. Geraldine is going through a period when all her sense of colour seems to have deserted her and has been known to wear Orange and Purple together. Ghastly. Ugh!

Apparently satisfied, the trunk lid was closed and they all got into the car, with Fatty in the driver's seat. We expected them to leave, but they sat in the car for ages. Shirley said it was only five minutes, but all this time we tried not to move, feeling we must be as conspicuous as snow on Ayers Rock.

"It's moving," whispered Geraldine and sure enough, it was. Slowly reversing, the car turned into the fringe of the plantation, and then pulled out onto the track again, heading in the opposite direction, towards the road.

"See if you can tell which way it turns off into the road," said Shirley, breathlessly. I knew how she was feeling. I had taken only about two breaths since we first sighted our visitors, but now we all sat on the soft grass and filled our lungs with the good, clean air.

"Wowsers," gasped Geraldine, "supposing they had seen us and had had guns. We'd be dead by now."

"Don't be so melodramatic," smiled Shirley, "Anyone would think they were crooks. Tell me what they were doing that was so wrong?"

I reminded her that anyone who could appear out of thin air, as they had done, was up to no good and why did they seem so suspicious when they got back to the car.

"They turned right," said Rachel, "towards the Ballarat road."

Bless her, we'd forgotten all about that. Chances were, that they had come from Ballarat, but of course, we couldn't be sure. The other direction didn't go anywhere in particular until it got nearer to the border with South Australia.

"What a pity," said Geraldine, "that we didn't get their registration number. We could have found out who they were from that."

"Well," mused Shirley, "we do know that it was registered in New South Wales, if nothing else."

Geraldine was mystified.

"How on earth do you know that?" she asked.

"Easy," smirked our little know-it-all, "When they reversed into the trees, I saw that the number plate had black figures on a yellow background and I know that the only state that has plates like that is New South Wales."

I wasn't happy. That's an understatement, I was very unhappy. I couldn't understand how they had suddenly appeared out of thin air and I said so.

"I'll show you," exclaimed Shirley and set off across the scrub.

Now we were all mystified. How does this shrimp know all these things that we don't? There didn't seem to be any place of concealment between our boundary and the pine plantation, certainly not enough to conceal three grown men, but as we neared the place where they had appeared, I suddenly saw a slight depression, in which were growing a number of stunted blackberry bushes.

Even when we stood right at the edge of the depression, I couldn't think why three men would bother to hide there. The depression was roughly dish-shaped and seemed to be no more than a metre deep at the most and the tops of the bushes were just below the surrounding ground level. Then I looked closer and I saw a much blacker shadow than the sunlight was producing and I realised that between the bushes, was a much deeper hole

Of course! This was another of the abandoned gold workings; one of those, about which we had been warned; one of those, which were deep enough to be of danger to unwary children. Of what interest could it be to our intruders? Already I was beginning to think as Geraldine was. These people were a threat to our ordered lives. Then my ears began to tingle and I knew that this was the start of another exciting adventure.

There were no obvious signs of any activity at all, so they perhaps weren't working the mine, but there must have been something here, otherwise they wouldn't have paid us a visit. Up till this moment, no one had spoken, but now Shirley broke our silence.

"I knew this one was here, because Dad warned me about it."

At that, there came from the bowels of the earth, the most wonderful sound I had heard all afternoon, the excited 'yapping' of an Australian terrier. We had found Boots!!!

Chapter 3

————— ⟨∘∕∘∕∘⟩ —————

Discovery

Somewhere down there, beyond the black hole, which was all we could see, was a happy little dog. I know that bark so well It's the one I hear every morning when I go out to the stable to say 'good morning' to him. The problem we now had to face was twofold. How far down was he and how were we going to get him up again? Shirley was on the ball again.

"That's why those men appeared so suddenly," she exclaimed, "because they came up out of the hole. So it must be pretty easy to get up and down."

"Easy for them," grumbled Geraldine, "they were grown men."

"It will be easy for us too," mused Shirley, "because they seemed quite neat and clean to me. Not like someone who has had to scrabble out of a hole in the ground."

There were no trees within easy reach of the shaft, but there was one hawthorn bush with a stem of about 5 cms in diameter and that is quite strong enough to support the weight of even the heaviest of us. I volunteered to go first to see what lay beyond the screen of the scrub bushes. By this time, since we were out of the direct rays of the sun, our eyes had become accustomed to the gloom and I could see that about a metre down, was a narrow shelf, from which grew a lot of blackberry bushes and hawthorn shrubs. Geraldine, who is the stronger of us, grasped the stem of the hawthorn bush with one hand and I took the other hand and lowered myself down onto the shelf. So far, so good.

I wondered about my Guardian Angel. Dad says I must tax him awfully, sometimes, because I am such a 'tomboy' and always getting into scrapes. I wondered if today, he would have to take drastic action on my behalf. I put my trust in Jesus when I was seven years old and I know that as long as I do my best to do what He wants me to, He will keep me safe. It's wonderful to have such confidence in Him. I knew that if I slipped from this shelf, the very least that could happen to me would be a broken leg or an arm, since I didn't know where the bottom of the shelf lay, then the worst that could happen, didn't bear thinking about.

"Can you see the bottom," whispered Shirley, "and can you see Boots?"

I knelt on the shelf and peered into the darkness. As I stared, the darkness seemed to melt and I began to see detail all around me. There was the bottom, not quite flat, about five metres down, but no signs of a little dog. There was no shortage of sound though, for Boots was barking his little heart out, just off to my left.

Then I saw it! In the left hand wall, a tunnel had been dug into the side of the shaft and it was from this tunnel that the frantic yapping seemed to come. If Boots was in the tunnel, I thought, something was stopping him from coming to us. What could it be?

Geraldine was down beside me now and it was she who found the way down. Beginning right at my feet, was a crude ladder of stakes, driven into the wall of the shaft. They were about fifteen cms in diameter and stuck out from the wall about forty cms.

"Do you think they're strong enough to carry our weight?' she asked.

"Of course they are," answered Shirley, who was down with us now, "they must have been strong enough even for 'Fatty'."

We helped Rachel down onto the shelf and in loud whispers had a family conference. Geraldine was all for going back to fetch Dad, but even Rachel disagreed with that idea. This was OUR adventure and at that time, we really didn't think that we were exposed to any danger. None of us likes to think that we need grownups and we certainly hadn't up till now, so we decided that we would carry on and rescue Boots all by ourselves. Geraldine is always telling Dad and Mum that she should be treated like an adult now that she is thirteen years old and Dad is always telling her that she will be treated like an adult when she starts to behave like one. He generally follows this up by telling her to go and clean up her room, or finish her homework, or whatever it is that she's trying to get out of doing.

We came to the conclusion that since Boots is my dog and since I am the lightest in weight, (Shirley eats too much.) I should be the one to test the ladder and see if we could get down easily, also, more importantly, to see if we could easily get back up. Especially since one of us, probably me would be carrying a dog on the return trip. He may be a small dog, but he would need at least one hand to hold him. What was bothering us all, was why Boots didn't come to us. I could tell from his 'voice' that he was quite unharmed. He's a terrible baby and puts up all sorts of a fuss if he even has to have a scratch dressed, but now his bark was full-blooded. Dad says it goes through him, like a knife and I must admit, it is a bit piercing, but it didn't sound muffled, so that seemed to rule out a fall of earth. This time it was Rachel who had the common-sense answer.

"Why don't you go down and find out for yourself," she laughed," instead of hanging around up here and talking about it?"

Accompanied by much advice and encouragement, I grasped hold of the top rung of the ladder and put my right foot on the second rung and it 'gave' a little, but it was driven well into the wall and supported the weight that I put onto it. Now I placed my left foot on the third rung and brought my right foot down beside it. All of my weight was now on the ladder and I bounced a little, with no obvious results. Encouraged by this, I gave a hefty bounce. Rachel screamed.

"Careful, you'll fall, then we'll have two of you to get out and you're likely to be much more trouble than Boots."

Sweet child I thought, but nothing happened. Now I was very confident and finding that so far, the rungs were set at equal distances down the wall, I continued down into the gloom of the shaft, until I stood firmly on the floor, looking up. There was not much of the open sky visible from the bottom and my sisters were simply black cutouts with no recognisable features.

"Is there any water down there?" Shirley wanted to know.

"I'm not coming down there if there is," groaned Rachel, "You know what trouble I get into if I get wet feet."

We do indeed. It seems as if she spends weeks in bed with coughs and colds. There was no water. It hadn't rained in days so in less time than it takes to tell, we were all at the bottom of the shaft ready for the next stage. By now, we could all see quite well in the gloom, which in fact, didn't seem to be gloom any more.

First, we carefully searched all over the floor of the shaft for any hazards and finding none, made straight for the tunnel. There was a step up into the tunnel and then it sloped down slightly into the earth and ran for about ten metres, getting darker as we went, until almost without noticing it, we came to an obstruction in the shape of a gate made from slats of wood, nailed to a frame. Behind this barrier, yapping as if his heart would burst with joy was Boots.

He was obviously sound in life and limb and while I comforted him through the gaps in the slats, the others took stock of the situation and examined the gate, carefully. I must say, someone had been very clever. A heavy wooden frame had been made and had been fastened with large metal spikes to the wall of the tunnel, which at this point, had been made smooth and square so that the frame fitted closely and without any gaps. Then a sort of loose door had been made with slats, but this was not hinged as a normal door would have been, but was fitted over two large metal pins, one on either side of the frame, with brass padlocks through holes in the pins, to stop the door being taken off the pins. Without the key, or keys, to the padlocks, there was no way we could get to Boots. He was a prisoner until such time as someone could think of another way out of the situation.

I began to wonder why Boots had been locked up. Was it an accident, or was it important? No, I thought, the important thing was to get him out and get well away from this place before the men, whoever they were and whatever they were up to, came back. It was Geraldine who came up with the answer.

"We had a talk last week, about the Aboriginals up in Arnhem Land," she told us, "and one of the things I remember, is the terrific amount of digging they do with just a simple digging stick We could have Boots out of there in no time at all, if we can find a few sticks."

"But isn't this a rock floor?" asked Shirley.

For once, she hadn't known the answer, but a quick examination showed that the floor of the tunnel was nothing more than packed earth. I raced up the ladder and soon returned with an assortment of sticks for digging. Having no knife with which to shape a cutting edge, we had to make do with the way things were, but we soon got the hang of it and found the best edges of the sticks to dig with. When we began to scoop out the loose earth from under the bottom of the door, Boots, from the other side, must have thought we were after rabbits, because he began to dig furiously from his side of the barrier.

It didn't take as long as I thought it would and soon we had a hole big enough for Boots to wriggle out. What a joyful reunion it was with each of us thoroughly licked on every inch of us that was exposed. Such giggling and shrieking had never been heard in these parts before.

"O.K. gang," laughed Geraldine, "let's go before Captain Teach and his pirates return for their buried treasure and make us all walk the plank."

"That's just it," said Shirley, "I don't think I can go until I know what they are up to. What's so important that it has to be locked up like this? Maybe it is buried treasure and another thing, why did poor old Boots have to be locked up anyway?"

I agreed with her. I just had to know too. It was a matter of very little time to enlarge the hole under the gate until it was big enough for all of us to scrabble through one at a time. Now we really had an adventure on our hands. At the best, we were guilty of trespass and would be at the mercy of Dad's anger and possibly that of our local policeman, Senior Constable Patrick Muldoon. At the worst, we could find ourselves involved with a gang of drug pedlars or worse. It was too late to go back now, but none of us could anyway. We were committed as soon as we dug under the frame. The tunnel only continued another ten metres before ending at a 'T' junction.

"Which way?" queried Rachel.

"Right first," answered Shirley.

I'm sure she only guesses, but just around the right hand corner; we found what we were looking for. It was a box, about forty five cms long, twenty five cms wide and thirty cms deep It had a rope handle at each end and had no fasteners of any sort, being screwed together at all joints and without any lid that could be seen. It was painted a drab olive green and on the side, which was uppermost, was stencilled in white paint, the letters and numbers, PNS.13784 Mk. IV.

"It's something to do with the Army," confided Shirley, "because of that paint. No-one else would use a gungie colour like that."

"Courtney Dirk painted his garage that colour, Geraldine objected.

I knew that was true, but it was only because he bought the paint cheaply at the Disposal Store in Ballarat. However, it was a safe guess that this box was somehow connected to the Government. I realised now, looking back, that we all desperately wanted it to be so. Rachel poked at it very gingerly, with one finger.

"Bang!" shouted Geraldine.

We all jumped and Rachel shrieked.

"I bet it's enormously heavy." she said, when she could speak again.

Geraldine took hold of both handles and tested the weight.

"It's no heavier than my school books," she winced, "lets take it home with us."

Another long conference took place and the rights and wrongs of removing other people's property, were fully examined.

"Since it most likely belongs to the Government," stated Shirley, "and since our visitors are not your average looking Government representatives, then I think we have just as much right to the box as they do."

"Anyway," piped up Rachel, "finders keepers; losers weepers."

Unarguable logic from one so young, I thought. Geraldine wanted to blow it up and claimed she knew how to make guncotton. A little knowledge is definitely a dangerous thing, especially where Geraldine is concerned. What we did in the end was, I thought, rather clever, even if I, who thought of it, say so myself. We simply took it with us when we went back under the frame of the barrier and buried in the hole that we had dug to get under the barrier. When we had finished and the earth had been rammed firmly down, you couldn't see a mark where we had been digging and the surplus earth from the hole, we scattered over the floor of the shaft and trod it down.

"We must remember to take the digging sticks up with us when we go," Shirley reminded us, "it's little things like that, that give amateurs away."

We climbed up on to the shelf and disposed of our sticks in the brambles, and then Geraldine gave Shirley a boost up into the hollow from which the shaft had been dug.

"Just have a quick sweep around the horizon for any pirate ships," she quipped, "and if the coast is clear, we'll set sail for the Spanish Main."

Up went Shirley to the rim of the hollow, but she was back again in a matter of seconds, as white as a sheet.

"What's wrong with you, Shirley?" asked Rachel, "you look as if you'd seen a ghost."

"Worse than that," gulped our great brain, "there are two of the men coming back across the paddock. By now, they can only be about thirty metres away and they're coming fast."

Chapter 4

Trapped

Quickly, we scrambled back down the ladder and flattened ourselves against the side of the shaft nearest to where we thought they would appear. Our situation seemed hopeless for if they had come back to go down the shaft again, then we were bound to be discovered.

In a matter of seconds, we heard them slide down to the shelf and then begin to descend the ladder. I began to pray that God would protect us and Geraldine and Rachel told me afterwards, that they had both prayed that same prayer. Now it was up to God, for all that we could do, would be of no avail.

It's easy for me to laugh about it now, because it seems so funny, but at the time it happened, we were all paralysed with fear. The first man to reach the bottom, set off straight away for the tunnel, but the other man lost his footing as he stepped off the ladder and threw out his arm to touch the side of the shaft to steady himself. His hand grasped Geraldine's arm and she screamed, naturally. He jumped a metre in the air and screamed louder than Geraldine but he recovered quickly and placing himself at the foot of the ladder to stop anyone going up, he switched on one of those large torches that clip onto the top of a big square battery. As the shaft was flooded with light, he called to the first man.

"'ere, 'arry, look wot we 'ave 'ere." he chirped.

If ever there was a Cockney Sparrow, this was he and I immediately christened him 'sparrer'.

"Stroof," he said, "yew frightened the livin' daylights arter me. I 'ad nao idea there was anybody darn 'ere."

Arry, I mean Harry, was there now and he was a different kettle of fish altogether. I have never seen a meaner looking man in all my life. Neither of them was above thirty years old, but Harry looked as if he had suffered every day of his thirty years. Not so Sparrer, who was literally beaming, as if he had discovered a long-lost branch of his family. Harry grabbed Rachel, who was nearest to him and viciously twisting her arm up her back, spoke for the first time. His voice was cultured, but savage.

"Come on now," he rasped, "what are you up to and what do you know?"

Up till now, Boots had been quiet, but now he growled, ominously and I saw the hair on his back, bristle with anger. I had only seen him like this once before, when Ivor Robbins, one of Dad's deacons brought his Bull Terrier round one day. Fortunately, the Bull Terrier had decided to ignore Boots, but I had to give Boots full marks for true grit.

"'ere, it's Percy ennit?" said Sparrer, "Where on earf didja get 'im from then? I fort we got rid of 'im."

At the sound of 'Percy', Boots turned to look at Sparrer and I swear he raised one eyebrow. He really has the most expressive face of any dog I have ever seen and it was obvious that he knew Sparrer and it was equally obvious that he didn't think a great deal of him. He stopped growling though, which didn't help our situation because I was starting to think that if Boots would have a go at one of these intruders, then in the confusion, I might get away and go for help.

It was Shirley who answered Harry and in a simpering, childish voice, like nothing I have ever heard her use before, she laid the basis for the story we were all going to use, with various embellishments.

"We're gold miners and we're going to carry on where the old miners left off and when we've made lots of money and are rich, we're going to send a Missionary to Africa".

Doesn't she have an imagination? I'm sure I don't know which side of the family she takes after.

"'ow much 'ave yer farned so far?" chirped our little Sparrer, "and 'ow long 'ave yer bin at it?"

I suppose he really wanted to know how long we had been around the mine and whether we were likely to have seen anything, but Shirley was up to that one, bless her.

"Ever since lunch-time." she replied, "but we haven't had time to do any digging yet, so we're doing a survey first".

"And what," growled Harry, "has your survey revealed so far. What have you found, in other words?"

While all this was going on, my mind was wrestling with the sudden knowledge that Boots somehow knew these men, but only vaguely. Boots is an affectionate dog and if he had had a close association with them, he would have been all over them like a rash, as the saying goes. Still, he must have known them because he was now quiet, but still distrustful and a word from me, I fondly hoped, would send him at their throats. I decided to try.

"Sic!" Out of the corner of my mouth.

No response at all.

"Kill!" Sotto voce.

"Rats!" Hissed from the depths of my collar.

That did it! He went berserk. He seemed like ten dogs, all of them large and malevolent. He was everywhere at one and the same time and in the confusion; I managed to get as far as the third rung up the ladder. The noise continued, but just as I was praising the Lord, an iron fist grasped my ankle and I looked down into the face of Harry, which was twisted into a wry grin.

"If you were innocent, my dear," he drawled, "You had nothing to fear. Now I know that you have been up to something. Clement, lock them in the cage, until we find out who they are and what they have found out."

Clement! It was so out of character that I almost laughed out loud. Geraldine lacked my self-control.

"I knao," chirped Sparrer, "it aint my fault. It's me Mum see. She 'ad delusions of grandoor. Me Dad wanted ter call me 'Bill', same as 'im. I never 'ad nao say in it."

"Shut up," barked Harry, "and get on with it."

Sparrer produced a key, from of all places; a watch chain, which had a large turnip watch, attached to it and unlocked both padlocks. He pulled the gate from the pins and stood it against the side of the tunnel.

"In yer gao. Look lively. Any more for the Skylark?" It seemed that very little disturbed this perky little man and in spite of the circumstances in which we found ourselves, I was beginning to like him. He couldn't be all bad I thought.

We had no chance to do anything more than go before Sparrer into the tunnel. We stood there uncertainly, while Rachel rubbed her arm. I don't think Harry hurt her badly, for he didn't twist it half as hard as I do. It was probably just a nervous reaction.

"Check it out while you're there," said Harry.

"Wowsers." I heard Geraldine breathe.

So she might, for now we were in real trouble. Sparrer came back a lot slower than he had gone, but his face spoke volumes. I've since thought that the Apostle Peter must have had the same look on his face when Jesus came to them in the boat, walking on the water.

"'ere, 'arry," he croaked, his voice breathless with shock, "it's gorn. It aint there nao more. It's bin took ennit?"

Harry spun round, his face vicious as he snarled.

"Gone? How can it have gone? Check the other spur."

He faced up to Geraldine, who he rightly judged to be the elder and seizing her hair in his left hand, bent back her head. With his face literally an inch from hers, he spat out the words.

"If you have interfered in any way, with my property, girly, you will come to regret it. Far better to tell me now what you have been doing here and what you have done with my property."

'Sparrer had returned and he didn't need to speak. After a swift glance at him, Harry tightened his grip on Geraldine's hair.

26

"Well?"

It's at times like this that I most admire my elder sister. Generally she's wet, because she's getting to that age when she doesn't know if she's fish or fowl. Is she a woman, or is she still a girl? Is she one of us or has she crossed the line and become an adult? However, she didn't let us down this time. Although she was scared and she let him see that she was, I knew that she had control of herself.

"We came looking for gold, Sir," she gasped," but we haven't got anything to dig with, so we couldn't do much, could we?"

Harry's whole frame was distorted with rage, now. He was really a very bitter man. His face showed that he was no stranger to frustration and bitterness. Deeply etched lines bore evidence of rage and hatred. Oh, how I wished that I could tell him about Jesus, that lovely one, who could give him the peace that he had never known.

But I judged that this was not the most convenient time, while his hand was still clutching the hair of my sister.

"Up here," he spat, "bring 'em up here."

Under the strain of his vile temper, his cultured veneer was starting to slip. Geraldine was dragged up the tunnel and into the left-hand spur and the rest of us followed docilely behind, shepherded by the now quiet Sparrer.

"Up agin the back wall and daont move." snarled Harry.

"Wot, 'arry?" whispered Sparrer, apprehensively, "wotcher gonna do? Remember yer temper an' daon't do nuthin' yer'll be sorry abart."

"Get out of here," ground out Harry and as he did so, he kicked at a piece of timber that formed the side of another frame supporting the roof of the tunnel. Suddenly, with horror, I realised what it was he was going to do He was going to remove the prop, which would cause the roof to collapse so even if we weren't killed at once by the fall, we would be sealed up until the dead are raised. Even as I began to pray, the first rock began to fall and then, with a roar like thunder, the whole of the roof collapsed and dust shut out all the light and even sight of each other. If my sisters were still alive, like me, they were imprisoned forever, in a tomb of rock.

Chapter 5

⟨⊙/⊙/⊙⟩

The Mysterious Stranger

When the noise of the falling rock and earth had stopped, the first sound I heard was the quiet sobbing of one of my sisters, quickly followed by the joyful prayer of Geraldine as she realised that at least two of us were alive. A quick check proved that we were all alive, including Boots, but not all in good spirits. Geraldine continued to pray and thanked Jesus that we were all still alive and uninjured and as soon as she did, we recovered our composure. Dad always says it takes a lot to keep the Howard family down.

The dust had settled now and by feeling our way around, with much giggling as we encountered each other unexpectedly, in the dark, we gathered together in a group. I was all for starting to dig ourselves out through the rock fall, but Geraldine called for a council time and we all sat on the floor, in a circle, holding hands.

"It's no use just starting blindly to dig," said Geraldine, "we might start at the widest part and dig for ever."

"What we must do first," said Shirley, "is explore the rest of this tunnel and find out where it goes to. It might lead to outside again."

That was sound advice and so we joined hands and set off down the tunnel, feeling carefully, every inch of the way, both walls and floor. It was slow work, but it didn't take very long, for after a slow turn to the right, we came to the end of the tunnel. We established that there were no more offshoots and that the floor ran slightly downhill,

29

into the earth. At the end, the tunnel had been opened out to form a small chamber and the roof was just high enough for the average man to stand erect.

"I'm fed up," sniffled Rachel, "lets hurry up and get out of here. It will soon be time for evening service."

She was right of course. It must have been at least half past five and Mum would be getting the light tea that we normally had before church. They would be expecting us to arrive at any minute, bursting with life, expecting to be fed. That was one of the things in our favour. Dad knows his family and if we were more than half an hour late for tea, he would be out looking for us. I was pondering on the similarity between our earthly father and our Heavenly Father and finding many things indeed that were similar. The Bible teaches that God knows every hair on our heads and that He loves us all deeply, especially those who accepted His Son, Jesus, as their Lord and Saviour. I know that Dad loves us very much too and while he may not know every hair on my head, he often startles me by the way he seems to know even the way that I think. Mum told me once, that when we were quite small children, Dad would sit by our beds at night while we were asleep and he would pray for us and ask God to take good care of us. She said he would just sit, often for a long time, and then he would gently touch our cheek and steal silently out of the room. Oh, I just know he loves us so much.

"Look," yelled Rachel.

"Don't be daft," snapped Geraldine, "how can you look in this pitch blackness?"

"That's just it," yelped Rachel, "it's not pitch black. I can see smoke or something, going up a crack in the roof."

By giving careful directions, Rachel was able to concentrate our attention on what she had seen. She must have eyes like a hawk, for what she had noticed, was the final wisps of dust from the rock fall which were, indeed, going up through a crack in the roof. She was quite right to be excited. Mr Brown had told us one day in class, that without light, we could see nothing, for there were no visible rays for the eye to pick up and the brain to register. Therefore, if we could see the dust down here, then there must also be some light to illuminate the dust and if there was light down here, no matter how little, then it must be coming in from outside and the way was open to freedom. Perhaps!

We rushed to stand beneath the spot where the dust appeared to go up through the roof and as our eyes became accustomed to the change in light, we saw a large fissure and saw that there did seem to be a way out, if we could only reach it. We were only about six metres below the surface and when Harry had caused the tunnel to collapse, because we were so near the surface, another shaft had been opened up where the rock had fallen. This one was not vertical however, because the fall had slipped sideways and our new shaft had a bend in the middle and it was because of this bend that most of the light was shut out.

"It looks wide enough," said Shirley, "At least it does as far as the bend."

"That's the trouble," groaned Geraldine, "what if we get that far and then get stuck. We'd never get found and we'd starve to death."

You see what I mean about Geraldine being 'wet'. That's the way Mum thinks. We were going to starve anyway if we didn't try to get out.

"If," said Shirley, always the practical one, "Elaine stands on Geraldine's shoulders, she should be head and shoulders into the hole. All she has to do then is scramble up."

It seems that the present combination of my age, size and weight, is just what is necessary to get me the rough end of all the scrapes we get ourselves into. Geraldine is too heavy to stand on anyone else's shoulders so she has to be the one on who's shoulders we stand. Rachel is light enough to stand on anyone's shoulders, but even on Geraldine's shoulders, she's too short to reach anything and Shirley falls into the same category. Once again, I was the 'patsy'. Still, it was my life too, so I guess I had no choice.

Standing on Geraldine's shoulders was no great task. I'd done that many times before; doing it in the dark was the catch. By the time

I'd managed, we had wandered half way down the passage and had to be led back by Shirley while my head bumped all along the top of the tunnel. When we finally found ourselves underneath the fissure and I was able to stand up straight, I found that I was more than head and shoulders into the new shaft. I could see now, that there was only one bend in the shaft and I guessed that once I got round that, then as long as the shaft was wide enough, it should be easy to climb up and go for help.

As I stood there, looking for my next handholds, I was suddenly conscious of two changes. The light coming down the shaft seemed to be flickering like an old movie and there was a scuffling noise above me. Then, before I could even give any serious thought to what it could be, I was struck on the head by some object, lost my balance on Geraldine's shoulders and fell in an untidy heap at her feet.

"The roof's falling in." screamed Rachel.

I didn't think so. The object that had struck me on the head had not been heavy. It was the shock that had caused me to lose my balance and not only that, now that I thought about it, it hadn't been hard either. Not like a rock or a large clod of earth. I told them about the noise I had heard and the flickering light and they all had theories about the cause.

"It was an Owl," said Rachel, "that lives in the crack and you've disturbed it."

Geraldine didn't go for that.

"Don't be a nut, Rachel," she smiled, "there wasn't any crack until Harry made one a few minutes ago. I think it was just the earth settling down after the disturbance."

"Not acceptable," voted Shirley, "I've been scuffling about in the dark with my foot and I can't find a thing on the floor, anywhere."

At that precise moment, Geraldine screamed and my blood froze in my veins, as the saying goes.

"Something hit me in the face," she yelled, "Wowsers, I've got it. It's a rope. Someone's dropped a rope down the new shaft. Who can be up there?"

Secretly, I hoped that it was Sparrer. I clung to the belief I had had that there was good in him and I really hoped that the Lord would honour the prayer that I had been praying, that the Holy Spirit would work in Sparrer's heart, to bring him to a knowledge of his need for Jesus in his life. I didn't know who would tell Sparrer, but I knew that if God had heard my prayer, and I knew that He had, then someone would be found who was willing and able to carry the Gospel to Sparrer.

Geraldine pulled on the rope and decided that it was fastened to the top. In no time at all, I was back on her shoulders and now that I had the rope, it was really easy to get to the bend in the shaft. I wedged myself across the shaft, using my back and my knees, while I thought about my next move. Predictably, it was Shirley who came up with the answer.

"It's like climbing up a chimney," she said, "not that I ever have, but if you turn sideways to how you are now, you can go up and over the rock, then you can turn back the right way again."

She was right, of course, I could and I did, then in no time at all, I was up the rest of the shaft, which was even wider at the top and out into the light and beautiful clean air. Quickly, I looked around, hoping to see Sparrer, longing to thank him and tell him about Jesus. Sparrer wasn't there, but I did catch a glimpse of someone. Two hundred metres away, just too far to be really recognisable, stood a male figure. Even as I saw him, he turned and walked into the pine plantation.

Goodness me! Was I seeing things? A Swagman! A genuine, old-time Swagman, complete with bottle corks around the rim of his broad-brimmed, felt hat. Trousers roped at the knees and his swag on his back. I cried out to him, but his only response was to increase his pace until I could no longer see him. I was tempted to follow him; to plead with him to help me to get my sisters out of what would have been our tomb, if Harry had been successful, but the cry of Geraldine from the bowels of the earth, brought me to my senses, it would be far better to get them up, out of there, before there was another fall of rock.

Geraldine just made it with Boots. When at last, she stood beside me, gulping air in as if she had just discovered that breathing was going to be banned from now on, she resolved to eat less in future. With Shirley and Rachel, it was much easier. We simply tied a loop in the end of the rope, in which they could put a foot, then together, Geraldine and I, hauled them up like sacks of coal, pausing only while they eased their way round the bend in the shaft.

When at last, we were re-united on safe ground, we stood with our arms round each other and we let Rachel thank Jesus for our deliverance. Some day, before she gets much older, I'd love for you to hear Rachel pray. Dad says she beats all the theologians into a cocked hat. She talks to Jesus just like she talks to her Teddy bear, so matter of fact; so certain of her communication; so secure in the love that exists between them. One of Dad's deacons will do anything to get out of hearing Rachel pray. He always weeps and blows his nose, very loudly, like a trombone. I like him and call him 'uncle Con'.

You'd think that after all we'd been through, we'd be more than keen to get back home and tell our parents what had happened, but we all decided we must go back to the main shaft and see if there had been any developments. We were reasonably sure that Harry and Sparrer had left the scene of their crime, so we wasted no time in climbing back into the old mine shaft and picking our way, gingerly, up the tunnel. When we reached the barrier, we learned the worst. Beneath the bottom member of the frame, which had contained the gate, was a gaping hole. Our carefully planned and meticulously executed scheme for hiding the box had been blown and the box was gone.

Chapter 6

Enter the Police

Somehow, it seemed a dreadful anti-climax. If the last two hours of suffering were to count for anything at all, then at least we should have been able to return the mysterious box to it's rightful owners, whoever they may be. We were all agreed on this.

"Without that box," sighed Rachel, "I can't believe any of this is real."

"Dad won't believe us anyway." groaned Geraldine.

"We'd better keep quiet," said Shirley, "at least until we hear anything about it. We'll sound real Charlies if there's nothing to it at all."

"There's no doubt in my mind," stated Geraldine, "I can still feel the pain of Harry, hanging on my hair. I don't think I imagined that for a minute."

I agreed with Geraldine. If Harry and Sparrer were innocent, then there was no explanation for their behaviour, especially that of Harry.

We set off home in complete silence. Even Rachel had nothing to say and each of us was completely lost in the happenings of the last two hours, as we turned over in our minds a kaleidoscope of events. As we reached the end of the barn, Shirley must have raised her eyes, because she stopped dead in her tracks with a gasp.

"Mr. Muldoon's here. It must be later than we thought and Dad's sent for the police."

I didn't think so, Mr. Muldoon knows our family and he knows us. He has been involved at the tail end of some of our adventures before and I was quick to point out that he would be very unlikely to drop everything and run round to Dad at the first inkling of anything wrong. He once said that we would always turn up, like the proverbial bad penny. We had to explain that to Rachel and when she got the message, she was very much on her dignity. Just before Mr. Muldoon left, he felt a tug at his sleeve and found Rachel at his side.

"Senior Constable Muldoon," she piped, "we will always turn up because we trust Jesus to keep us safe and He will never desert us."

Mr. Muldoon, who is a good Catholic, said it wasn't right or fair of us, to impose such a burden on the good Lord and may He forgive us. Nevertheless, there was the white Holden Commodore that represented the Law in these parts and the blue lamp on the roof made it official.

"G'day," he said, "y'look as if yer well jest ran dry."

"Where on earth have you been?" said Dad, "you're absolutely filthy."

We looked at each other and it was true. Our shoes were thick with mud and our clothes and hair were grey with dust from the cave-in and where we had wept with relief, wide rivulets had been washed through the grime on our cheeks. We looked like the children of Israel, after forty years in the wilderness. Dad took a closer look at Rachel, who can't keep anything from being written on her face and saw there, sufficient to cause him concern.

"You'd better come in again, Pat," he sighed, "I feel that somehow, no matter how unlikely it may seem at present, my family are concerned with what you have been telling me."

We all trooped into the family room and Dad stood in front of the fire, where he always stands when he's going to lecture us on our shortcomings or over-indulgencies. Snr. Constable Muldoon sat on the arm of the settee and we all sat around on the floor. Mum came in from the kitchen.

"Where on earth have you all been," she sighed, "you're absolutely filthy."

Geraldine grimaced at me and Shirley said that Dad had said that already. Dad got down to it straight away.

"Geraldine," he was smiling and he's at his most dangerous then, "have you seen any strangers around this area in the last few days?"

We exchanged rapid glances and in them was the realisation that this was no longer our adventure alone and that we had to own up and face the music. I saw Geraldine's faint shrug and knew that she had accepted responsibility to deal with this situation.

"Yes Dad," she whispered, "we saw three today."

"Perhaps Norman," said Mr. Muldoon, "you would allow me to continue?"

Dad sat down in his armchair and Patrick Muldoon moved to the fireplace and became the inquisitor.

"Now girls," he began grimly, "on Thursday last, two men broke into a small factory in Melbourne, which is operated by a division of our Commonwealth Scientific and Industrial Research Organization. A third man, waited outside in a white Ford Falcon. To all intents and purposes, the factory makes instruments for hydraulic systems and it's never been thought necessary to guard the place. I'm sure you'll agree, that that's one good way to draw attention where you don't want it. Anyway, the men have stolen something of great value to the security of our nation and it's vital that we get it back before it falls into the wrong hands entirely. Now we know one of the men; he's a toolmaker from England, who worked at the factory for a time and therefore knows what really goes on there. We also know that he has relatives in the Ballarat area and his vehicle was seen in Ballarat on Saturday, but not since. All the Police Officers within a radius of fifty kilometres have been alerted to keep a watch for this car. If you have seen it, or anyone you don't know, around here, you don't need me to tell you, that you must tell us now, what you have observed."

That was a long speech for our Patrick and we all sat and stared open-mouthed at him. He hasn't had so much to say since Wendell Brown tricked him into appearing in the school pageant last year. He thought it was going to be a walk-on part, until he accepted, then he found out he had to learn a half page of script about the struggles of the early 'diggers' on the goldfields. It was some performance and for months afterwards he had to live with all sorts of wisecracks from the local larrikins, which did nothing for his image as the up-holder of law and order.

The sudden attention un-nerved him, for he subsided quite suddenly onto the settee and began to fiddle with the buttons on his shirt. Mum spoke quickly.

"Geraldine, you said you saw three men today. Do you know who they were? And where did you see them?"

I knew exactly what Geraldine was thinking and as I looked across at Shirley, I knew that she was thinking the same. We were so close to this whole thing now. We knew two of the three men very well indeed and knew what they were up to. We were in a splendid position to track them down if they were still in the area and solve the mystery all by ourselves. It would be foolish to tip our hands now, before we at least had a go at bringing the criminals to justice. With a warning glance at Rachel, Geraldine spoke.

"We saw them over by the pine plantation. They looked as if they had been into the plantation for firewood."

Clever girl. Not a lie exactly and we did get a few 'townies' who came out for the dead pine trees, not realising that the resin from the pine smoke, can choke up your flue in a matter of weeks.

"Did you see what sort of a vehicle they had?" said our worthy Constable.

Have you noticed how the police always talk about vehicles? Never about cars or trucks; always vehicles.

"What's he mean?" hissed Rachel.

She has a very loud stage whisper.

"I mean," said Patrick, patiently, "did you see what sort of motor car they were riding in?"

"Mr. Muldoon," said Rachel, equally patient, "I don't know one motor car from another. They all look alike to me."

Dad knows this one. He calls it prevarication or some such thing.

"Shirley," he said softly, "don't tell me they all look alike to you too. Did you see it?"

"Oh yes," simpered Shirley, "I saw it."

"Well?"

"Well what, Daddy?"

"Well, did you see what colour it was?"

"Yes Daddy."

"Well what colour was it?" Not so softly now.

"It was white, I think, Daddy. Yes, it was white."

Dad was wondering whether or not to continue this line of questioning, since Shirley too, is a past master at the art of prevarication. Since Mr. Muldoon was here, he obviously thought that he should continue.

"Tell me my dear," smiling again, "did you happen to notice what make and model the car was?"

Shirley noted the smile and knew that Dad wasn't kidding. The time for plain speaking was now upon us.

"It was either a Ford Falcon," she said, "or a Nissan Bluebird. I can't always tell the difference unless I see the back of them."

Dad looked at Mr. Muldoon in triumph but Mr. Muldoon wasn't so sure I could see doubt written all over his face and even in the way he was slouched down in his seat.

"The Forestry Commission has got a white Bluebird," he sighed, "it could easily have been theirs."

"On Sunday?" queried Dad.

"Yair," said Patrick, "Jim's bin after a feller who's snaring rabbits. He's bin doin' a fair bit of damage lately and Jim said he'd get him, if he had to stay up all night to do it I guess that would include Sundays too."

"But," remarked Dad, "Geraldine said there were three of them. There's only one of Jim."

Patrick saved the day for us this time.

"He told me on Friday, that his two brothers were coming up for the fishing and that between them, they'd sort this poacher out and they would too; great strapping fellers. Did I ever tell yer about the last time they came up and about Kevin's pig?"

Snr. Constable Muldoon had lost interest in us. Dad knew he had and that he wasn't going to take our sight seeing any further. Dad hadn't lost interest, but he knew he wasn't going to get anywhere with us while Patrick Muldoon was about.

"Tell me about it, while I walk you to the car," he smiled, "and you girls, get cleaned up and ready for church I'll just about get there in time to preach the sermon. Rose, if you are ready, perhaps you would go on and ask Ben Livingstone to lead the service and that I'll be there in time to preach."

There was no way in which we could escape the inevitable. When we came back from washing and tidying, Dad was waiting for us in his study. When we go in there, we know he means business. We sat in a row along the old church pew he keeps for families who come 'en-masse' and waited for him to speak.

"Perhaps you had better speak for the group, Elaine," he started, "at least you can put several statements together concerning the same subject, without getting tied in knots."

He also knows that he can trap me into making statements that contradict each other and that I then give up and confess all. I could almost hear Geraldine and Shirley groaning. I played for time, pleading that the afternoon had been so crowded with excitement that I found it hard to marshal my thoughts.

"Well," smiled Dad, (there it was again) "I don't have too much time. Perhaps at least, you could make a start by telling me some more about the three men *you* saw."

My problem was simple. I had to put Dad off the scent for as long as it took us to wrap up the case of the stolen 'whatever it was', but I must not lie to him. This was one of the rules of our game that we would never break. I believe that to a certain extent, both our parents entered into this spirit but there was no way that we could ever be dishonest with them. The tension was terrible. At any minute, I knew that Dad would make me lose my composure. I need not have been concerned. It was Shirley who blew the whole scene. "Daddy", she pondered, "how do you open a box with a lid that has no hinges and no fasteners at all"?

Chapter 7

Shirley Has A Brainwave

The atmosphere was electric. You could have heard the proverbial pin drop into a pile of feathers. Dad cleared his throat.

"Where," he said icily, "have you seen such a box, I wonder?"

Where indeed, I thought. Had Shirley given up so soon? We all looked at her and the variety of expressions was very amusing. I knew I must have been smiling although no one else was. Dad was at his very sternest and poor Mum just looked bewildered. Geraldine's mouth was wide open; Rachel's chin was on her chest, but Shirley looked as inscrutable as the Sphinx.

"As a matter of fact," she said brightly, "I've seen quite a few of them. There's half a dozen at least, in the disposal store in Ballarat, but I've seen some quite recently around here, but I can't think where it was."

"But what made you think of them," asked Dad, "No-one had mentioned anything about boxes. Now what do you all know about this robbery?"

"Well," smiles Shirley, "it seems to me that if this thing that has been stolen is highly scientific and valuable, like Mr. Muldoon says, then they would take great care at the factory to protect it against accidental damage. It would have to be in a box of some sort and I always associate those boxes with the government because of the awful colour they paint them."

Mum smiled. She thinks Shirley is very smart and always defends her, whereas Dad just thinks she's cunning and always suspects that she's teasing him. There was a long silence while Dad digested this, then he scratched his head.

"I have seen something like that, he mused, "and somehow I connect it with the church."

"That's it," yelled Geraldine, "the Scouts; they have four of them and use them as Patrol Boxes and keep all their silly secret things in them. They think the Guides can't get in because they haven't got proper fasteners and hinges and things".

Well, he'd been successfully diverted it seemed and there were no more searching questions, but had he been put off the scent altogether, we wondered? Only time would tell, for Dad has a memory like an elephant when it suits him.

On the way to church, we managed to have a few words in private and decided that after the service, we would go straight into the church hall and see if the boxes were the same as the one we had seen.

"We may," said Geraldine, "be able to use one of them as a substitute some time, if we have to, if they are the same and of course, if we ever find the original box again."

"That's a point," said Shirley, "they're probably on their way to Red China, by now."

I've never known such a long service. Normally, they simply fly along. I just love to hear Dad talk about Jesus. I can almost reach out and touch Him as He moves amongst us. My favourite time though, is the 'sharing time' when people tell of the way He has blessed them in some way, during the past week. He's been so good to those who love Him and keep His Word. Many times I find it hard to hold back the tears that sting my eyes and often, I don't even try. But on this night, I was impatient to see what was going to happen next.

Dad always leaves the pulpit just as the people are singing a final chorus and makes his way to the door, so that he can greet everyone as they leave, but this particular evening, we were out before the chorus began and slipped into the hall before he had a chance to see us. The hall was in darkness and we didn't dare to switch on any lights because the main windows face the front of the car-park and the light would be seen from where Dad stands to talk to the people However, we knew from experience, that he was going to be at least thirty minutes.

"Can you find them in the dark, Geraldine," whispered Rachel, "It's awfully spooky, isn't it?"

"I could find them in my sleep," giggled Geraldine, "We've put so many toads and dreadful things like that, in their precious boxes."

Little did we know the surprise that was in store for us, when we found our way into the small room that 'Skip' uses as his den. The window of this room is opposite the back porch of the church and the porch light shone feebly into the room, but provided enough light to see quite clearly, the various items of furniture and the Troop gear that was stored there during the week, when other groups used the hall. There were the boxes, neatly stacked in one corner. There wasn't enough light to tell for sure, what colour they were painted, but enough light to read the names of the Patrols, painted on the sides of them.

"Owls," read Rachel, "Kookaburras, Wombats, Echidnas........ who's is the one without a name?"

"Owls, Kookaburras, Wombats and Echidnas," said Geraldine, "that's all there is. Just four Patrols".

"Then why," demanded Rachel, "are there five boxes?"

"One, two, three, four, five," counted Shirley, "she's right."

There certainly were five boxes, near enough identical in size, shape and colour.

"It's probably Skip's," explained Shirley, "he needs somewhere to keep his gear, I suppose."

"He has his desk," said Shirley, "he has too much stuff to keep in a silly little box."

She was right, naturally, but I was already taking down the fifth box, which had no name printed on it It was heavy, but with the rope handles, which they all had, it wasn't difficult to get it down onto the floor and turn it round. There, on the top, which had been against the wall, was the stencilled legend 'PNS.13784. Mk. IV.

"Wowsers," gasped Geraldine, "Thar she blows. We've struck oil, right on his nose."

That's my sister. Talk about mixing your metaphors. Anyway, she was so excited; I had to let it pass. We had, by pure luck, located the missing box and all we had to do now was to call Dad and as far as we were concerned, the adventure would be over. The same thought must have occurred to all of us at the same moment. We were on the horns of a dilemma.

"Perhaps," suggested Rachel, "one of us could wait here until they come for it, then we could follow them to their hide-out."

"You've been watching too much television; too many old films," laughed Geraldine, "They don't have 'hide-outs today. They 'lay low' in Motel units until the heat is off.

"But," said Shirley, "didn't you hear Mr. Muldoon say that one of them had relatives in this area. If the whole family are crooks, then they could lay low at the relative's house. That's why they are up here in the first place, because they had family to go to until the heat is off."

She was absolutely right once again, but what was worrying me, was who this mysterious relative was It seemed to me that it had to be someone who was connected with our scout troop, in order to get the box into Skip's den. At the very least, he had to be able to get hold of a key somehow. The others hadn't thought of this, but now, as they did so, the same terrible thought occurred to them.

"It hurts me here," groaned Rachel, putting a hand to her chest, "to think that anyone who comes to our church could be a thief."

"Bless you, Possum," answered Geraldine, "but it isn't that simple. It's easy enough to borrow the key to the hall on the pretext of looking it over to see if it's suitable for a particular function, then while you still have it, you simply get a duplicate key cut."

"But," whispered Shirley, "some-one had to know that the scouts had those boxes in the first place."

"That cinches it, I guess," sighed Geraldine, "but who on earth could it be?"

I thought that this would be a pointless exercise, since out of our population of about nine thousand, there are three hundred members of our church, four more connected to the scouts and guides and then all the families associated with the scouts and guides. That's a lot of people and we had to find some means of identifying the one, or ones, who had taken advantage of us to use our church hall to conceal their crime. Shirley liked Rachel's idea, until Geraldine told her she could be the one to wait, then she had second thoughts.

"Why," she said, "don't we all wait?"

"Because," laughed Geraldine, "we could wait here until we starved to death and they still might not come."

"But if we don't stay," worried Rachel, "they'll come back and take that box away again, then we'll never know where it is, We can't be this lucky again".

"That's true," pondered Shirley, "but what if we take it first?"

It seemed so simple, until we came to think of where to hide it. We couldn't take it out of the hall, in case some one saw us with it and there were too many possibilities in the hall for us ever to agree. Finally, we did agree however and we hid the box inside an old radiogram with no works, which the scouts had brought in from somewhere and we made sure that we didn't disturb any of the months of dust which had accumulated on the cabinet. We were counting on adult people expecting a radiogram to be full of wires and valves and things. I think we planned well, as you will see.

"We'd better get out, quick," cautioned Geraldine, "before Dad misses us and decides that we're up to something. We have to be doubly careful now that they suspect we know about the affair. Anything we do that is out of the usual is going to seem suspicious to them."

Dad was waiting for us when we got back, but he didn't have much to say, except to ask where we had been. Rachel answered first.

"We've been round to the back of the church to look at the stars."

"You must have remarkable eyesight," remarked Dad, "there's heavy cloud tonight."

"That's why we have been such a long time, Dad," explained Shirley, "we were waiting for a break in the clouds."

We were silent on the short journey home, each of us, Dad included, was occupied with his or her thoughts. Dad was the first to speak as we were walking up the path to the back door.

"I'd like to know who that Englishman's relatives are. I thought that I knew everyone in Olney, but of course, they could have been settled here for years. You can never tell about people."

No one answered him. None of us wanted to start a conversation that we couldn't handle and right now, there were far too many aspects of the business that didn't make sense to us and that was dangerous ground. Dad could so easily lead us into an area where he could trap us in a bad mistake. When we had had time to analyse all our thoughts, then we would be able to take evasive action and pursue the criminals to the bitter end. We knew that Jesus would never leave us, or forsake us and if we entrusted this to Him tonight, in prayer, then He would lead us to the solution and along the way, would also keep us from harm.

We went to bed as soon as we could and I knew that each of us, including little Rachel, would spend some time in prayer before settling down for the night. As for me, it was late before I got into bed, but I fell asleep quickly, tired from the day's events, the excitement and the unusual mental activity, but secure in the knowledge of Jesus's love.

Chapter 8

Foiled Again

The next day, being Monday, we were all back at school again and I was very tempted to talk to our Head Teacher, Wendell Brown and seek his advice. He's so sensible, for an adult that is, also I felt that I could trust him to keep our secret. When I talked to Geraldine at lunchtime, she was totally opposed to talking to anyone about it. She thought that the merest breath of a rumour in the town, would get back to the crooks and in the end, I had to go along with this opinion. It does seem that any whisper that's dropped at one end of the town, finds it's way to the other end with the speed of a bush fire. Geraldine had been doing some thinking and I was impressed.

"The scouts," she said, "always meet on a Tuesday night, don't they?"

I agreed that this was so. That's the way they want it.

"Well then," confided she, "whoever put that box in the den, will have to come back for it before the scouts meet again So it will have to be done before tomorrow night and since they dare not risk going into the hall in daylight, then they must come tonight."

I didn't think this was necessarily so, because if our mystery relative was a local man, he may well be someone who is entitled to use the hall during the hours of daylight. Still, we had to start somewhere and that seemed to be a good place to begin.

On Monday afternoon we have Maths and English, my two favourite subjects, but this day was the longest I have spent in my entire life to date. I just couldn't wait for school to finish so that we could have a council of war. Because of Dad's commitments with discipling new converts, we have an early meal on Monday evenings, so by six thirty we were finished and by seven o'clock we had the dishes washed and put away No one had any homework, so we were free to pursue our own interests.

A council of war was called in Geraldine's room and everyone was there including Timothy We never try to shut him out of our plans, firstly because he's our brother and we love him and secondly, if we make a fuss about him being there, he just hangs around and becomes a nuisance. We find that he soon gets fed up with what he calls 'girly talk' and leaves after a few minutes anyway.

We opened our meeting with prayer. First Geraldine prayed for wisdom for us all, and then Shirley prayed especially for safety for the whole family.

"You hear such terrible stories from America," she told us, "about children being kidnapped to stop their parents doing something to bring criminals to justice. Wouldn't it be simply awful if Dad and Mum were parent napped to stop us from trapping Harry and Sparrer and Co?"

I thought it would be easier to stop us by kidnapping us, but I didn't say so because it was a beautiful prayer and if that was what was worrying Shirley, then it was right that she should ask Jesus to take the burden from her. It's not right that Jesus should have paid the price at Calvary, for our sin and waywardness and that we should continue to carry burdens that He would willingly carry for us if we would only surrender them. Then Rachel prayed and we all wept. That child is too good for this world. She's an angel in disguise and the way she talks to Jesus is so precious. I feel that He's right in the room with us, in person I mean, visible and He's holding Rachel's hand and she's looking up into His lovely face and it's true what the hymn says, 'and the things of earth will grow strangely dim, in the light of His Glory and Grace'. He's a wonderful Saviour and we all love Him so much. It's difficult for me to stop writing about Him. I prayed that through all this rottenness, we might see the hand of God at work and that some good, however little, might come of it.

The next thing was to decide on a plan of action. We had to try to out-think them somehow. The crooks, that is and if we were seen going into the hall, then it was certain that no one else would go in while we were there.

"But," objected Shirley, "They have to get the box out before the scouts see it."

"The scouts won't see it," Rachel reminded us, "because we have hidden it in the old radiogram."

"That's true Rachel," smiled Shirley, "but Harry and Sparrer don't know that. All that they know is that they have to get to it before the scouts find out that they have one box too many."

"I've got it", yelped Geraldine.

"I hope it's nothing catching." giggled Shirley.

"Numbskull. I mean I've solved our problem. We'll take the spare key to the back door and go in through the school and the playground. There won't be anyone on that side of the school grounds at all after school."

That was perfectly true. After school was out, there was no need for anyone to be on the premises. Mr. Mac, the caretaker, does all the cleaning before school begins and only puts in an appearance after school if there is any maintenance to be done. It would be very bad luck indeed, if he were about, so it looked as if the coast would be clear.

By eight o'clock we were in the hall and installed in the 'loft' where the scouts keep all their tents, ropes and such gear. The big problem had been dear old Boots. There was no way we could have had Boots and secrecy, they are opposing terms, so he had to be left behind, but he didn't agree with that and raised Cain. He obviously considers himself a part of the family and where we went, he thought he should be too. Eventually, we locked him in Dad's tool shed, knowing that Dad would hear him there, as would half of Olney and that he would be let out, but by that time we would be long gone and Boots would never reason out where we were. It was sad in a way, because he does so love to be with us and into everything that we are into. I guess he's just very sociable.

The 'loft' is really the space above the den, which has a flat roof. The ceiling joists of the den have been covered with boards and it makes a very useful storage area. There's no light up there and that suited us just fine. We passed the time by examining all the possible suspects for the traitor amongst us. It had to be someone who was familiar with the coming and goings of the scout troop, yet we were all agreed that it couldn't be any of the warranted scouters. That was just too much to accept. Mr Livingstone, who is the scoutmaster, has been there for simply hundreds of years and is also one of Dad's deacons. Dad told me once that Mr. Livingstone was Skipper when Dad was a scout and that's before living memory. The Assistant Scoutmaster is Dudley Chadwick. Deadly Dudley we call him. He's only twenty and I can't imagine any way he could be involved in anything like this. His idea of excitement is to go down to the town centre and watch our only set of traffic lights change colour. That only left 'Bosun', who is sort of quartermaster, or secretary. Nobody knows much about him, but everybody likes him. We tried to imagine him as a crook, but we couldn't make it work. He's a local councillor too and I kept seeing him kissing babies, which he does with great gusto, at the Liberal Party Fete every year. Dad might know something about him though.

I was aroused from my reverie by Geraldine and Rachel, hissing simultaneously.

"Someone's coming. Ssssh!"

I listened. Two someone's were coming along the side of the hall towards the front door. We heard the jingle of keys, the metallic scratching as the key sought the keyhole, and then the squeak as the door swung open. None of us dare look, even to raise our heads. Again, we felt very exposed, since the loft had no front, so to speak and we relied for our concealment on the tents behind which we crouched and the deep pockets of shadow. Would they be bold enough to switch on the hall lights? I supposed that would depend on who they were. We were left in no doubt about this last point as soon as the door was closed.

"'ere 'arry, ennit dark? Shall we light a match?"

Harry didn't answer and Sparrer had no more to say as they made their way across the floor to the door of the den, immediately below where we crouched, holding our breath, lest it should be heard and willing our hearts to stop beating so loudly, for to us, the beating sounded like a mighty drum, in our ears.

The door of the den swung open and we heard their footsteps, as they crossed to the corner where the patrol boxes were stacked. Harry spoke first and his voice was clearly audible. I had wondered if we would hear through the ceiling, but there was no difficulty at all in hearing.

"Which one is it?"

He had regained his old composure and his polished British accent.

"'s the top un ennit?"

Sparrer was quite matter of fact. At this stage there was no reason for him to see any other picture than the one he had seen when he had placed the extra box on top of the neat stack of four boxes.

"Clement," said Harry, icily, "there is no top one. There are only four of them. Which one is ours?"

"Lemme look 'arry." quoth Clement.

Oh dear, I could never learn to think of him as Clement. Even if the Queen, for extraordinary services rendered to the Crown, should knight him he would always be 'Sparrer' to me. The chirpy little Cockney 'Sparrer'. There was a brief scumbling beneath us, then a short period of absolutely deathly silence, while the earth seemed to stand still.

"Aow, 'arry," groaned Sparrer, "it's gorn agen."

If I live to be ninety-seven, which is even older than Mr. Muldoon's mother, I could never describe, nor do I expect to hear again, such strangled fury as poured from Harry's lips. Poor Rachel had never heard anything like that and had never even suspected that people could be so angry. She said afterwards that she thought perhaps Sparrer had stabbed Harry and that Harry had gone berserk. Whatever she thought, she gave a little cry of anguish and jumped to her feet, knocking over one of the bundled tents that we had stood on end to conceal our presence. Had the loft been fifteen centimetres wider, the tent would have fallen flat and stayed there, with the possibility that it's fall may not have been heard, but as it was, the tent fell, overhanging the edge of the loft and there just wasn't sufficient loft floor to support it, so it continued it's fall and landed with a thud, right outside the door of the den. Now we really did hold our breath.

Out dashed Harry, closely followed by Sparrer. Harry flashed a rapid glance all round the hall, then upwards, right into the startled face of Rachel. We were sprung!! Standing up, we all went to the edge of the loft and looked down at the furious Harry and the sheepish Sparrer.

Harry's performance fascinated me. He had to be quiet of course, or he might draw attention to the fact that someone was in the hall, but it didn't restrict his anger one little bit. The fury and venom that he managed to get into one word was impressive.

"You!"

"Hallo, Mr. Harry," Shirley said brightly, "we're playing 'Hide and Seek', would you like to join in. You and Mr. Clement close your eyes and count to five hundred and then you have to come and try to find us."

I remember thinking at the time, that if they took us up on that offer, I would be in Western Australia when they opened their eyes. However, Harry didn't want to play.

"Get….down….here….at….once." he hissed.

Shirley was still keen to play 'Hide and Seek'.

"Alright, Mr. Harry," she said, equally brightly, "we'll count and you go and hide."

Harry couldn't speak at all now, but at last, Sparrer found his voice.

"I fink yewd betta come darn gels, the games up ennit?"

Chapter 9

This Time, You Die

Harry was calmer now, since he knew where his troubles lay. At least, one assumes that he now associated his loss with our presence on the scene; therefore he imagined that by bringing pressure to bear on us, he could reclaim the situation.

Shirley wasn't finished yet.

"If you don't like Hide an' seek, we could always play 'Shops'. There's plenty of stuff in here we could use in the shop."

Not a flicker betrayed Harry's thoughts, but Sparrer smiled.

"Yew gotta nerve, yew 'ave," he said softly, "I gotta larf."

"I don't think you realise," said Harry, "just what it has cost me in time, labour and money to get this far in the operation. Now I find myself balked at every turn by a pack of demented, giggling schoolgirls. Well, my patience is about run out and you only have yourselves to blame for what I am about to do. I have a deadline to meet; one more delay will put me out of business."

Although he spoke conversationally, I think we all detected the barely concealed menace in his voice and Sparrer flinched, as he too, recognised that Harry had had enough.

"'ere", he gasped, "yew carnt me art of ennythink vicious I tole yer from the start, I ent standin' fer nuthin' vilent."

"That's quite all right, Clement my boy," sneered Harry, "just help me get them back to the mine, then as far as I am concerned, you can go to the devil."

Sparrer thought about this for a while, then obviously considered it to be a good idea, since he grasped one wrist each, of Geraldine and Shirley and made for the door, Harry grabbed my wrist and Rachel's and followed.

"Make one sound," hissed Harry, "and we start shooting. Then someone you love may get hurt badly and permanently."

The car was at the end of the building and we were bundled unceremoniously into it. Three of us were wedged up on one side of the back seat and Rachel was sat on Harry's knees with her arm twisted up her back. I could see that she was in pain, but she certainly wasn't down for the count yet.

"I've been thinking," she said, "about what you said to Mr. Clement. About him going to the devil, I mean. You know, the Bible says that if we don't trust in Jesus, we will all go to the devil. I've trusted in Jesus and so have all my sisters and so has my little brother. Have you, Mr. Harry?"

Harry didn't answer and we had no way of knowing if he even heard her. Not by so much as a twitch of an eyebrow did he show that he was listening, or even aware that she was speaking to him. But Sparrer was listening and he had half turned his head towards her.

"Mr. Harry," she said, simply, "would you like me to pray for you? Then you can repeat the 'sinner's prayer' and ask Jesus to come into your heart; all your sins will be forgiven and your name will be written in God's book."

"All I want of God," said Harry, "is to stop your mouth, but since he doesn't seem to care, I guess I'll have to stop it myself."

We were now back at the track, which ran alongside the pine plantation and with all the lights turned off, we crawled to a point opposite the mine. With the help of 'Fatty', who never said a word the whole time he was with us, we were dragged back to the mine shaft and

58

half thrown, half dragged down the shaft. After bundling us back into the cage, the door was put back and the padlocks replaced and locked. We were prisoners again and our previous escape route was blocked by the fall of the tunnel. I felt that this time, the devil had dealt us a bad hand. Harry spoke again.

"I'm going to knock out the sluice gate which is holding back the water in the dam and in two hours, or less, this shaft will be under water. No one will hear your cries out here and no one will think of looking out here for days. By then, no doubt, you will know for yourselves, whether or not there is a God."

There's no argument at all, that amongst other things, Harry was an out and out sadist. He just loved to inflict pain on everyone, even his so-called friend, Clement.

"Don't do it 'arry," he said, "yew'll never find the box, if yer do."

He was much shaken and as white as a ghost. I thought again of the good I had imagined in him and I suddenly knew that the Holy Spirit had revealed that to me. How else could I have been so sure? Quickly, I prayed that through all this, Sparrer and maybe even Harry, would come to know that One, who could make all things new.

Harry drew from his inside jacket pocket, a short, squat little pistol and weighing it in his hand, turned to Sparrer.

"Coming," he said, quietly.

"Nar," said Sparrer, equally quietly, "best carnt me art."

It was like a snake striking, so fast did Harry's arm move. Afterwards, we could hardly say what he had done, but there lay poor little Sparrer, at his feet, as he slowly counted.

"One, two, three, four, five, six, seven, eight, nine, ten. Always glad to oblige. Don't mention it, old chap."

Then he was off, up the ladder and away.

There was a long silence and I became aware of the trembling of Rachel's small body. I put my arm about her and as she moved closer to me, she spoke the thoughts of us all.

"Poor Sparrer, now he will never know Jesus."

"He's not dead," said Shirley, "his chest's going up and down. That means he's still breathing, but he's got a nasty gash on his head where Harry 'pistol whipped' him."

Where does she pick up these expressions?

By now, we had all recovered a little of our composure and we began to take stock of the situation.

"It's going to take a bit longer to dig ourselves out without sticks, this time." said Geraldine.

I had to agree and then I thought, why hadn't Harry realised that we would simply dig ourselves out again? Examination of the bottom frame of the door showed us why. Long steel rods had been bent like large tent pegs and had been hammered into the floor of the passage, not only stopping us from burrowing underneath, but were effectively anchoring the frame to the floor of the tunnel. His background as a toolmaker had helped him make use of the available material and his skill had helped him to fashion the large pegs. That was one door that was effectively closed to us.

"We got out before," said Rachel, "where we least expected it. Let's have a look round and see if God has opened up any new doors for us."

It didn't take long to decide that all that was left to us was to start moving the rocks and earth that had fallen, when Harry had removed the props and to see if we could beat the rising water when it began to flow, as it surely, soon, must. We wondered how long it would be before Harry and Fatty were able to destroy the sluice gate and divert the water from the dam into the mineshaft.

A council of war was called and we all sat down, held hands and Rachel prayed, asking for great wisdom beyond our years, that we might be able to follow God's leading. We had exhausted all our own abilities and strengths and knew that if we were to get out of this pickle, it was only going to be because of His intervention.

It didn't help that it was now pitch dark, but we all set to and began to take what rock we could scratch out of the heap and transfer it to the other leg of the tunnel where the box had been stored. It was slow work and I for one, was thinking of all the possible alternatives. Maybe Boots had finally been let out of Dad's tool shed and was already looking for us. What could he do though, even if he found where we were? He couldn't get down the ladder to us, and even if he could and we were able to attach a message to him, he surely couldn't get out of the shaft again without help. Sooner or later of course, Dad and Mum would realise that we were missing and would come looking for us. After a reasonable time, they may call in outside help, but by then, it would be too late to help us. The shaft would be full of water and so should we.

The Apostle, Paul, said that to be absent from the body was to be present with the Lord. That being the case, I was sure that we were soon to be with Him. I tried to decide how I felt about that and had to conclude that although I trusted Jesus to take me when He wanted me, I didn't want to go just yet. I'd talked to Dad and also to Mr. Brown, about all the options that were open to Christian girls and was quite decided that before I settled down to marriage and domesticity, I wanted to spend some time in foreign mission fields. I have always been excited by stories of the mission fields and the adventures of Missionaries and still get a great thrill when I think about Gladys Aylward and her faith on the China missions. Both Geraldine and I have decided that we could do much worse than marrying a young Pastor and helping him to establish a growing church body.

I can honestly say that I can't think of anyone happier than my parents who have been serving Jesus since long before they were married. They live by faith, of course, our church being an independent one, with no other income than the tithes and offerings of it's people and Dad has never had to preach about 'giving'. You see, if you live according to the teaching of Jesus, then you can expect to receive all the rewards that are promised to those who keep His commandments. I feel very sorry for those who are outside the family of God and who think that 'religion' is all about 'thou shalt not'. Our church has an annual meeting of the members and one of the things that happens is that Dad's salary is reviewed. They ask him to step out of the room while they do it, but he's never out of the room very long.

All this time, we had steadily been removing rock from the fall, but I could feel that we had made little impression on the huge pile that had come down from the roof and walls of the passage. There were several large pieces that our combined efforts would never be able to move. It was a thankless task and I began to lose interest and to look around for other possibilities. So had Shirley it seems, because at that moment she gave a loud cry.

"Look at Sparrer," she yelped, "he's floating!"

It was true. He had been lying in a shallow depression with his outflung arms up on the rim of the depression, but now, the water had risen so high in the main shaft, that his legs and his lower body were gently weaving back and forth in the muddy water that was lifting his body. Even as we watched, his body slid slowly backwards down the slope and as his face went into the water, we heard the bubbles as he exhaled into the flood. His next breath would be inhaled and his lungs would fill with water. He was barely visible now, by the fitful light of the moon down the mineshaft and he was drowning.

Chapter 10

Desperate Hours

Sparrer's ducking was just what he needed, for with a splutter, he raised himself from the water and sat with his back against the wall of the shaft, coughing as if his life depended upon it, which of course, it did. In a few minutes he was breathing normally, although as yet, unable to speak.

"Are you all right," asked Rachel, "Would you like to borrow my hankie? It's not very big but it's clean in most places."

"Nar, I'm orl right. Blimey, wot an 'ead ache though, I feel as if me 'ead's bin blown up wiv a bicycle pump".

"You're funny, Mr. Clement," giggled Rachel, "Why doesn't all the air leak out again."

"At least," said Sparrer, "I won't sink in this water. I'll float fer weeks."

The water had been rising steadily all the time we had been talking and it was now up to Sparrer's knees and lapping over the lip of the passage and running down to the two spurs of the tunnel. Soon, as it continued to rise, it would become a problem to us and eventually, it would become the means of our end. It seemed to us that it would be a good time to prepare Clement for what would be the order of things when this happened. I asked him if he thought he would be going to Heaven if this should be the end.

"Lord 'elp yer Miss," he said, "nobody knows that fer sure, do they? I mean, I've done some wicked things an' I've done some good things. It aint fer me ter say, now is it?"

So I told him that the Bible was very clear about the way that God had decided this issue and I asked him if I told him how it was, would he like to do something about it?

"I bin finkin' abart wot this 'ere young gel said in the car," Sparrer said, "It keeps coming back ter me, see. Like it's stuck in me mind, ennit. Abart trusting Jesus. But, I wunt know 'ow ter go abart it."

"You haven't got very long to make up your mind," said Shirley, "the water's rising very fast now."

"'struth," gasped Sparrer, "can'tcher 'elp me?"

I had to be certain that he knew that without Jesus, he was lost. Dad says, so often, that nobody was ever truly saved, who didn't know that they were lost. So I explained what St. Paul had to say to the church at Rome, about everybody coming short of the standard set by God. He was able to understand that and see that even if he hadn't done any of the things that he said he had done, he would still be a sinner in the eyes of God because of his disobedience to God all the years when he had turned his back on Him. Then I told him what God said were the wages of sin. Sparrer thought that was fair and that he had never thought that anyone would praise him for some of the rotten things he had done.

After that, I told him that Jesus had died on the cross, so that his sins could be forgiven and that it would be unjust of God to punish Sparrer for his sins, after Jesus had already been punished for those same sins. Sparrer went very quiet and I thought at first that I had gone too far, too soon.

"Did 'e do that fer me?" he breathed.

I heard a sob, but it was not from Sparrer, it was my tenderhearted sister, Geraldine. Bless her, she can never hear of the deep love of Jesus without feeling corresponding love for Him. Then there was another sob and Sparrer clutched my arm through the gate.

"I never knew that," he sobbed, "why dint nobody never tell me?"

He continued to sob quietly to himself, his body heaving convulsively, as the sobs shook him.

"'e shun't 'a done that," he sobbed, "I knew I 'ad ter pay some day. 'e was too good ter die fer me."

"Mr. Clement, said Rachel, quietly, "God loved you so much, that He gave His only Son, so that if you would only believe in Him and what He'd done, you wouldn't have to die, but would have everlasting life. That's the best-known verse in the whole of the Bible and it's for you as much as anyone."

"'e shun't 'a done it," he repeated, "'e shun't 'a done it."

There was a long pause, and then he said softly,

"But I'm glad 'e did. What do I do next"?

Rachel prayed for him, for I couldn't. I was too choked up. So was Geraldine and so was Shirley. I've already told you how it is when Rachel prays, haven't I? This time was no exception and we all wept noisily. Then she led him through the sinner's prayer.

"Dear Farver," he sobbed, "I've done some awful fings an' I know that to you, even the good fings I done, don't add up ter much; but ternight, I want ter tell yer I'm sorry fer everyfink an' I want yer ter forgive me an' give me a new start. Yer kin see I aint much (he added that bit himself) but I wantcher ter know that I intend ter make a betta show of it wiv your 'elp. This 'ere little gel's one of yours. I kin tell, an' she sez I can arks yer to come an' live in me 'eart. I dunno if that's possible, but I wish it was, 'cos yer see, God, I carnt do nuffin right by meself. 'arry's always done everyfink for me that 'ad to be done. So I'm arksin yer God, ter do it if yer can. I want yer to. Right now. Will yer?"

Even Rachel was weeping now, but it was with joy for the lamb that was back in the fold.

"I wish everyone didn't weep when I pray," she whispered, "hardly anyone weeps when Daddy prays."

Deep in my heart, I harbour the suspicion that when Rachel prays, even Jesus weeps and in my more whimsical moments, I see God blowing His nose with a mighty 'trumpet' on a soft, fleecy cloud.

In the excitement of Sparrer's salvation, we had forgotten all about the rising flood, although it must have been creeping up our legs the whole time, for now, we found it to be up to Rachel's knees and we could hear it pouring down the wall of the shaft, in torrents. Shirley was most matter-of-fact.

"I'm sorry that we are going to die like this. I'd always fancied a deathbed scene, with all my family around me, hanging on my every word. This seems such an anti-climax after the excitement of the last couple of days."

"So did I," said Geraldine, "and when I've thought about it, Jesus always came personally to take me home."

I remember reading in one of Daddy's 'Reader's Digests' that many people have seemed to have had that experience and have actually cried out a welcome to Him. It told also, of one horrid old man, who on his deathbed, had cried out that a demon had come to fetch him, then fell back dead, with the most ghastly expression on his face. It must have put the wind up his family and scared some good behaviour into them for weeks afterwards

"Wot abart singin' some 'ymns ter keep our spirits up?" said Sparrer.

"I'm afraid I'm too cold to sing, Mr. Clement." said Rachel and I could feel her little body trembling against mine Sparrer insisted that she should have his jacket and although when he managed to get it through the bars of the cage, it was soaking wet, she put it on and gradually, she said, she began to feel a little warmer.

"Let's jump up and down on the spot," giggled Geraldine, "like we do in the school playground,"

"Don't be daft," said Shirley, "we'll just splash each other and get wetter than ever."

"That was supposed to be funny, Shirley."

Now Geraldine was cross too. Sparrer, with true Cockney humour, was determined to do what he could to raise our spirits and he splashed around in the water out in the main shaft, pretending to bump into all sorts of things. First it was a great white shark, then an iceberg, then a submarine and finally, he assured us he had found the Titanic.

It worked with Rachel and Shirley and soon they were laughing with great glee and joining in the nonsense.

It occurred to me, that there was nothing to stop him from climbing out of the shaft and disappearing forever, but obviously, in his newfound release from his old nature, he had decided to remain with us. It was a hard fact for me to face, that although he was prepared to stay with us to the end, it was within his power to save us by giving himself up and leading rescuers to us. But I needn't have concerned myself, for the Holy Spirit was already at work in his heart.

"I gotta go an' get 'elp." Sparrer blurted out.

"But you'll be arrested," gasped Geraldine, "and spend simply ages in jail."

"Someone must come soon," said Shirley, "why don't you wait a little longer, Just in case?"

"Naow," said Sparrer, "I've bin thinkin' abart wot 'e done fer me an' I jest know 'e expects me ter do the same fer all of you. 'e expects me ter give meself up fer you, jest like 'e did fer me."

"I'm afraid you're right Clement." said Shirley.

As usual, she had hit the nail right on the head. The water was now up to Rachel's chest and even if she climbed onto someone's shoulders, we were only delaying the inevitable. The choice was Sparrer's and no one could make it for him. Was he to give up his liberty so that we could be saved, or would he stay with us and watch us drown?

Chapter 11

—⟨∘/∘/∘⟩—

Here Comes The Cavalry

The silence that followed was long and strained. No one seemed to want to be the one who broke it, for conversation must bring decisions and none of us wanted to make decisions. Finally, it was Geraldine who spoke, softly and wistfully.

"Poor boots, he must have been locked in the toolshed an awful long time. What time is it Mr. Clement?"

Sparrer didn't answer for a moment, and then his behaviour startled us all.

"Time?" he shouted, "Time? I'll tell yer the time! The time, o' course! Stone me! Wot's wrong wiv me 'ead? Musta bin that bump ol' 'arry give me. Me watch! Where's me watch?"

As he struggled to pull his huge turnip watch from his pocket, the penny dropped for us all. We had all seen him take out his watch to unlock the padlocks, because the keys were on his watch chain. It took but a minute to take out the keys, find the padlocks by feel and unlock them. We were soon out of the passage and into the shaft, but this brought fresh problems. Rachel was now out of her depth and had to be carried by Sparrer and the water was lapping just below Shirley's chin. There was no time to lose.

Fortunately, the water was not entering the shaft anywhere near the steps and so, our way out was clear.

"This way," chirped Sparrer, "any more fer the Skylark?"

70

"What does he mean"? asked Rachel.

"It's an old English joke," said Shirley, "only understood by old English people."

"Funnee," said Geraldine, "lets get out of here."

"Plenny o' time," explained Sparrer, "don't panic whatever yer do. The little gel's all right wiv me, you others get yerselves art, smallest first."

We lifted Shirley onto the bottom but one rung of the steps and watched her safely to the top, then I went up and finally Geraldine. Then Sparrer helped Rachel up, step-by-step, following along behind, to make sure that she didn't fall back into the water. At last, we were all up on the rim of the shaft, exhausted by our ordeal, our exposure to the cold and wet and our final struggle up the steps to safety.

We lay where we fell, panting to regain our breath, until slowly, Rachel got to her feet.

"Mr. Clement," she said softly, "do you think you can get up onto your knees for a minute?"

"Yus ducks," he replied, "yus, I fink so."

He did so, without too much trouble and Rachel went to him, put her arms around his neck and soundly kissed him on his cheek.

"Yew didn't orter do fings like that." he said quietly, and I could tell that he was fighting hard to keep control of his emotions.

"Dint yor Mum tell yew not ter 'ave ennyfink ter do wiv strange men?"

"I want you to know," whispered Rachel, "that even if the whole world turns against you for the things you have done, Jesus has forgiven you because you asked Him to and I have forgiven you because you cared what happened to me enough to stay with me when you could have escaped. And, you helped me to get out of the mineshaft."

"That wasn't nuffink," he murmured, "an' ennyway, I 'adn't got nowhere to go after 'arry left me."

He got to his feet and we all followed suit.

"The fing ter do now," he said, "is ter get in an'ot barf an' straight inter bed wiv an 'ot water bottle."

We began to climb up out of the depression around the mineshaft, when Sparrer stopped short.

"'ere, 'ang abart, he exclaimed, "there's lights coming acrorst the paddock It could be 'arry coming back 'cos 'e carnt find the box."

But I had heard something too. A high-pitched, excited, out –to –catch-a-rat-or-something-like-it, yelp. Geraldine heard it too.

"Boots," she yelled, "Bo-o-o-o-o-o-o-ts."

We didn't see him, but we felt him. A high-speed ball of fur, quivering from head to tail, hit us at nearly the speed of light. His wet nose was everywhere and now he was too excited to yelp. He squeaked with joy.

Then Dad was there and somehow, he gathered us all up in his arms. He tried to speak, but couldn't and neither could we. In a moment or so, he found his voice, but it wasn't to us that he spoke.

"My God, my Father and my friend," he prayed, "I thank you that when I trusted you, it was with everything I have. Forgive me for ever having a moment of concern for the safety of my children. Nevertheless, I am grateful that you have returned them to me safely. From this moment I know that they are yours and that you have great things planned for them. Help me now to be a better steward over that which you have entrusted to me. I praise you and thank you, in the name of Jesus, Amen."

More hugs and kisses for everyone, from everyone. The other 'light' turned out to be Patrick Muldoon and during our reunion, he had taken Sparrer into custody and was quietly leading him across the paddock to our house, where no doubt, his car would be waiting.

"Daddy," said Shirley, "what will happen to Sparrer?"

"Who on earth is Sparrer?" said our father, sternly, "and will you please make an effort to speak properly. You know how I deplore the abuse of plain English".

"Sparrer," said Rachel, "is my friend, who saved me from drowning and he got his name because he's a Cockney Sparrow; bright and chirpy."

"Children," said Dad, "you know of course, that he is a habitual criminal and that he has stolen valuable equipment from our Government. You must realise too, that he is, to some extent, responsible for the predicament you were in."

"But Daddy," broke in Shirley, "while we were down the mine, he became a Christian. Elaine told him how, and Rachel led him through the sinner's prayer."

"It was beautiful, Daddy," piped up Geraldine, "he was really sorry for everything he had done and he couldn't understand why Jesus had gone to the cross for him."

"No," said Dad, "I don't understand why He died for me, but I'll always be truly grateful that He did. As for your friend Sparrer...I mean Sparrow, I'm afraid that the law will have to run it's course. However, his sentence may be reduced in view of his concern for his former victims. His three associates have already been arrested. They were caught in the Scout Hall by Jim and his two brothers. Jim thought they were the poachers he's been having trouble with up at the Forestry Commission and to make matters worse, they showed resistance and in the process, they got quite a mauling by those big brothers of Jim's. They'll be kept in custody tonight, then they'll be taken over to Ballarat for charging, I expect."

"Did you say 'three' associates," asked Geraldine, "I can only think of Harry and Fatty. Who's the third?"

"A man and his wife, moved here from Ballarat, two months ago and moved into old Mrs. Felgate's cottage and it seems that the woman is a cousin of one of the men. It also seems that Boots came with them because when Boots saw the man, he went for him like a tiger. Anyway, the man got a key off Mr. Mac, because he said he was thinking of hiring the hall for a function. Mr. Mac. said he lost interest when he found that we didn't allow alcohol in the hall. By then of course, he'd taken the key over to Ballarat and had a duplicate key cut."

I wanted to know what it was all about, but Dad said that Constable Muldoon was coming round in the morning with Major Harrison and that we were to take the morning off from school so that he could take statements from each of us before taking the men into Ballarat Police Station.

"Who," queried Geraldine, "is Major Harrison?"

"There seems to be some mystery about him," replied Dad, "but apparently, he is from another Government agency and was assigned to this case. Patrick says he saw him up in the plantation, dressed of all things, as a Swagman."

My Swagman! Now I would be able to thank him for his timely intervention when I saw him in the morning. I only had one problem now. How on earth was anyone supposed to sleep tonight, with all these unanswered questions?

Chapter 12

————— ❧ —————

Loose Ends

When dawn finally broke, it found us sitting on my bed, fully dressed, wide awake and waiting for it. It had been the longest night I had ever spent and my sisters had experienced much the same. It's always like this when an adventure has come to a close, whether or not it has been successful. It's not that it's an anti-climax; it leaves us with our nerves wound up and no way of relieving the tension. We've had lots of adventures before, but none of them ever moved as fast as this had. Going on past experiences, it's at least a week before we come down to earth.

There was no question of us having our quiet time with the Lord. We were wound up like clock springs and anything but quiet. We managed to thank Him for another day and to ask for peace, but we knew that nothing would change until Constable Muldoon and his visitor arrived and that could be any time.

Dad was up first and we heard him pottering about, getting Mum her cup of tea and it wasn't long before Timothy was up and about. He came into my room first and when he saw that we were all there, he wanted to stay and play games with us He has a very short attention span, so that he only stayed about fifteen minutes and he was off again. After Mum had had her second 'cuppa' she got breakfast for us all and we sat around the table together. Dad often says that the family that eats together stays together, so we make a big thing of always having every possible meal together. They always begin with Dad praying and asking God's blessing, not only on the meal, but also on everything we are going to do during the day. At least, all the things that we **know** we are going to do. There's not a great deal of conversation during the meal, but it's certainly not discouraged, as it is in some families we know. The best part, excluding the eating of course, is the discussion we have at the end of the meal. I may have said before, that no subject is barred as long as it isn't frivolous. Today however, Dad said that we were going to wait for Patrick and Major Harrison, because he said we would have to go over everything twice, if we didn't.

What an agony it was, waiting. Mum said a watched pot never boiled and Rachel went over to the cooker and said it wasn't even turned on, so how could it boil? Shirley tried to explain, but I don't believe she got anywhere.

Our visitors arrived about nine-thirty, when we were all like cats on hot bricks. Patrick said that he'd been on the 'phone all morning to his superiors in Ballarat and his final instructions were that he was to bring us and the prisoners over to Ballarat, because we were considered to be 'material witnesses' and he had to get Dad's permission to do so. They were going to send the divisional bus over for us and some extra policemen to make sure that the gang didn't attempt to escape. Dad agreed to our going and said that he would liked to have gone himself, but he had some visiting to do, which he must get done before Sunday, or he'd be in real trouble.

"Well," said Patrick, "let me introduce Major Harrison to you and he can tell you what we already know and you can maybe fill in any gaps that you may see as we go along."

"All you need to know about me," began the Major, "is that I am a serving officer in the Australian Defence Forces and currently attached to A.S.I.O. I'm sure you know that that organisation is responsible for the safety and security of us all and that much of what it does is highly secret. As for this affair, no doubt you young ones know almost as much as we do, but we'll work on the assumption that you know nothing and I'll tell you all that I am allowed."

He took a deep breath and began.

"The evil genius behind the whole affair is a man called Harry Ashley, a toolmaker from England He came out here in 1968 because, he says, he couldn't make a go of it in England. My honest opinion is that anyone with a good trade like that, who couldn't make a go of it there, was unlikely to do any better here, or anywhere and that seems to have been about the size of it. He reckoned that the Australians and even the other English migrants had got it in for him and I think that has something to say about the type of man he is. He's a malcontent, pure and simple. He hadn't got a police record in those days, so that when he applied for a job with C.S.I.R.O., there were no problems. When they knew he was trained in the U.K., they snapped him up. For a time, all went well, and then he began to get into trouble. He began to lose interest in the job and several important projects were seriously delayed because of faulty work on his part.

Finally, he was given the customary Australian warning. Shape up, or ship out. Well, he did shape up sufficient to keep his job, but he was never any good after that. He resented the fact that he had been tried and found wanting. He could never believe that others didn't think he was as good as he thought he was. The next seven or eight years must have been purgatory for him, for like all of us, he craved attention, but he never realised the advantage he had in his skills and so he never got the recognition that he could have had. He became bitter and disgruntled".

"What's disgruntled," asked Rachel, "Can you get gruntled as well as disgruntled?"

"Don't interrupt, my dear," Dad exclaimed, "unless you've got something really important to add. Otherwise we'll be here all day."

"Quite right, Norman," chipped in Patrick, "Carry on Major."

"Where was I?' asked the Major, "Oh yes, I remember. Well, eventually, he reached the end of his tether and just before they could sack him, he disappeared last week with the fourth of a series of Artillery Sights which he had been working on. This particular one, is a 'night-sight', which is able to magnify the very small amount of light which is available at night and enables the gun-layers to 'pin-point' accurately, their targets."

"P.N.S. Mark IV." murmured Shirley.

"What did you say, Shirley?" said Dad.

"I said P.N.S. Mark IV," she replied, "which I think means Project Night Sight, number four. There was a number too, but I don't remember what it was."

"And where," asked Patrick, "did you see such a nomenclature?"

"I thought Major Harrison said it was an Artillery Sight?" queried Rachel.

"Rachel, my dear," said Daddy, "would you please try to curb your natural curiosity about things unknown to you, until we have heard all there is to be heard. You may make notes if you wish, but please, do not hold us up any further."

"Thank you, Reverend Howard," said the Major, "where was I? Oh yes, where did you happen to see those particular letters and numbers, in that particular order? Incidentally, you were perfectly correct." he referred to his notes, "The nomenclature which was stencilled on the box was P.N.S. 13784 Mk. IV. and it means exactly what you guessed it to mean. Now, do you know where that box is at this moment?"

"No." said Shirley.

"Oh." said Patrick and his face fell a mile.

"But, said Shirley, "I know where we put it and if Harry and company didn't find it, then it *might* still be there."

"Presumably," said Dad, "they were looking for it when Jim found them and if they didn't have it with them when they were arrested, then it must still be where the girls hid it."

We all trooped over to the hall and when we went in, my heart leaped within me, for the old radiogram had been pulled away from the wall and now lay on its face. They had found it! Then, as I ran across the hall, I could see that the back had not been taken off. The weight of it when they had turned it over, had suggested to them, just as we had hoped that it would, that the insides were still there, inside and they had been too slipshod to check properly. It was a matter of seconds for

Patrick to pry off the plywood back panel and there, for all to see was the vital evidence that a crime had indeed been committed. There was P.N.S. 13784 Mk. IV. in all it's drabness.

"All's well that end well, said Patrick smugly.

As if he'd had anything at all to do with it. There it was, the awful unfairness of being what the world calls 'a child'. I doubted if we would get any credit at all, for our part in the recovery of one of our nation's secrets, but it was thanks enough that whatever else we had blundered over or into, we had at least, managed to save the gun-sight from being stolen.

"Were they going to sell it to a foreign power?" asked Geraldine.

"Ashley said they hadn't made any plans," said Major Harrison, "but that he favoured selling it back to the Government, but I doubt if he could have carried it off. He seemed to be totally inept. He wouldn't have been able to get as far as he did, without his two more professional accomplices. I was coming to them. One of them, Clement Dakins, seems to be really taken with you girls. He was quite concerned that you may have caught a chill last night. We've checked his record with D 24. and he's a born loser. Petty crime all his life and nearly always caught in the act. He's been in jail more than he's been out of it and this time, he looks like he's going down for a long time."

"Is there nothing that can be done for him, Patrick?" asked Dad, "He repented last night and has made a statement of faith in our Lord. It seems a great pity that he shouldn't have the same chance that we all had when we repented."

"Ah," said Patrick, "there you have the rub of it. When we repented, in most cases the Police Courts were not involved. There was only God to forgive us. In Dakin's case, it's not so straightforward. In all his previous convictions, he never asked for forgiveness, nor expressed any remorse. If there is any possibility that he is genuine in his conversion, then there is every chance that he can be rehabilitated after he has served his sentence."

"What about the other two men, Mr. Muldoon?" asked Rachel.

"Arthur Bayliss and Gilbert Johnston are related by marriage. Neither of them has any previous record."

"Never done bird." Said Shirley. She really is remarkable.

"Never done bird?" exclaimed Dad, his voice rising in pitch, "What on earth do you mean, Shirley?"

"It's Cockney rhyming slang, Dad," answered she, "Bird lime; time. Time in her Majesty's prisons."

"Thank you Shirley," replied Dad, "I'm much obliged to you for your translation."

I asked if it would come out in court, how Sparrer had been knocked down by Harry because he wouldn't go along with Harry's evil plans and how he had stuck with us even though he knew it would lead to his arrest.

"It wouldn't normally," said Patrick, "because it's not pertinent to the case, but I'm very impressed with that aspect and I intend to bring that up when I give evidence as the arresting officer."

I'll skip over the next hour which Patrick spent taking statements from anyone who came near him. I feel that he would have liked a statement from Boots too, signed with a muddy paw-print, but he had to be satisfied with statements from Dad, Mum, Geraldine, Shirley, me and Rachel. Major Harrison said he would give him one later, but as he went out of the room, he winked at me. I don't think that Patrick is going to get a full set for his office files.

When the police bus arrived, we got on first and were taken right to the back seats. Then we went round to Patrick's house where he has an office and a single 'lock-up' and the prisoners were brought out and put at the front of the bus. They were handcuffed to the handrail on the top of the seat in front of them. Three of them were surly and refused to look anywhere but at their feet, but one of them, who we would now only acknowledge as 'Sparrer', looked round at us and grinned.

Before any of us could stop her, Rachel was out of her seat and alongside Sparrer. She touched her little hand to his cheek.

"Sparrer," she whispered, "I love you and I'm going to be praying for you. Please give Jesus a chance to help you. He loves you too and He can do so much more than I can do."

I saw the policeman who was behind Sparrer, swallow a big lump, then he said,

"Sit down please Miss; the bus is going to start now".

Quickly, she returned to her seat and turned to look out of the window, but not before we saw the big tears that silently ran down her cheeks. The journey to Ballarat took very little time and that time passed in silence except for the noise of the bus and the passing traffic outside.

When the bus reached the Police Station in Camp Street, the prisoners were taken into the cells and we were taken to talk to a senior officer who asked a lot of questions. He was by far the nicest policeman I have ever met, except for Patrick and he was very interested in all that we had to say about Sparrer. When I asked what would happen to him, he said that Sparrer would have to go to jail.

"The law must take it's course," he said, "and justice must be seen to have been done."

He thought however, that if we spoke up in court as we had done today, then the court would pay due attention to what he called 'mitigating circumstances' and it was possible that the court would be as lenient as it was able.

That was yesterday.

Today, in school, we found ourselves the centre of great interest, but opinions were divided. There are those who think we made up the whole story. They are the ones who are badly informed, but they will learn differently as time goes by. In our community, everybody eventually knows everything. There are a few idiots who say we are really members of the gang, but, because Patrick is our friend, we were let off, but whatever anybody thinks about us, we are very grateful to God for giving us, not only a wonderful adventure, but also the opportunity to lead a sinner into the loving arms of a tender Saviour.

No date has been set for the trial yet, because the courts are so crowded, but the four men who tried to steal the secrets of our Government, purely for gain, will inevitably face a jury of their peers. It seems a foregone conclusion that they will all be found 'guilty as charged' and be sentenced to a term in jail. We are praying that Sparrer, that loveable Cockney mongrel, will throw himself, not only on the mercy of the court, but on the mercy of the Saviour too.

The end.

Lightning Source UK Ltd.
Milton Keynes UK
UKHW011058180820
368429UK00001B/130

9 781648 033018